CAMPUS CONFESSIONS

xo Ronette

Book 1

JEFF GOTTESFELD

SADDLEBACK
PUBLISHING

CAMPUS CONFESSIONS

XO Ronette: Book 1

Frenemies: Book 2

Choices: Book 3

Crush: Book 4

PUBLISHING
www.sdlback.com

ISBN-13: 978-1-62250-701-6
ISBN-10: 1-62250-701-0
eBook: 978-1-61247-952-1

Printed in Guangzhou, China
NOR/0713/CA21301218

17 16 15 14 13   1 2 3 4 5

*W*ith thanks, to Saddleback.

Chapter One

If Jayson Jones hadn't had such damn fine guns, my life would have been a whole lot easier.

I'm Ronette. I have a last name—Bradley for what it's worth—but my hotel nametag just says Ronette, because last names don't matter when you're an eighteen-year-old high school graduate cleaning rooms to make a little chip. All my boss wanted was for me to do my quota of rooms as fast as I could so the Chicago Apex Airport Express didn't have to cough up any extra hours at minimum wage.

Let me say this: it sucked to be cleaning rooms at a two-star hotel when my fine boyfriend with the amazing guns was headed off to college the next morning. He wasn't going to just any college either. He was going to Houseman University in Washington, D.C. Houseman is what they call a "historically black college and university," also known as a HBCU. It's a great school with a mostly-black student body. I applied there and didn't get in. More on that soon.

I was proud that he was going to Houseman, but it was also scary. The Houseman University girl-to-boy ratio is two-to-one. Two sisters for every brother. It's that way at a lot of HBCUs. If our men paid more mind to their grades and less mind to getting into a sister's pants, that ratio might equal out. Not that I was in any position to talk about minding my grades. I'd finished Corman High School in the bottom third of the class. I know. Pitiful.

My GPA didn't get me into Houseman. In fact, it barely got me into Chicagoland Community College, where I was to start in three weeks. Everyone says CCC got its name because C is a high grade for the kids who end up there. My mom, Kalina—I don't have a dad or brothers or sisters, just Kalina and me—wanted me to study dental hygiene. I wanted to take writing. Kalina said writers starve. Since Kalina knows a thing or two about starving, there was good reason to listen to her.

Meanwhile, my boyfriend with the killer guns was heading to college two weeks early. He had a football scholarship and the players arrived early for practice. Jayson is six foot two and built like the star running back he is. In contrast, I'm short and skinny, with a cup size that would be a letter between *A* and *B,* if such a letter existed.

Jayson is caramel. I'm lighter. His eyes dance. Mine are dark pools. He keeps his hair buzzed. Mine is long and brown and goes with my swooping neck that makes people wonder if I'm from East Africa. His face is square. Mine is long. His voice rumbles. Mine is musical.

He's rich. His daddy is a Chicago alderman who some say will be mayor. His family lives in a penthouse north of the Chicago River. I'm far from rich. My mother works for the same hotel chain where I am a maid. She is a desk clerk and has done it long enough that her last name is on her badge. We have a furnished two bedroom near the O'Hare International Airport, one of the busiest in the world. All my life she'd worked for airport-area hotels. I had lived near takeoff and landing flight paths for so long that when I needed to fall asleep, I counted engines roaring the way other people counted sheep.

So, about that last night with Jayson before he went to Houseman … if he hadn't had such damn fine guns, it would have been a lot easier. Heading into last night, I'd sworn I'd stay a virgin until at least my eighteenth birthday. Maybe longer.

Ha. Lead me not into temptation. I can get there by myself.

Everyone says your first time is supposed to be wack. Either it hurts, or you don't feel anything, or the guy drools, or his member didn't remember what to do. It happens in a backseat or a locked room at a party where Pac Div pounds and your man's boys laugh in the hallway and wait for the blow-by-blow. So to speak.

It was not that way for Jayson and me. I hate reading sex scenes and can't imagine writing one, so I'll sum up my first time with Jayson in four words, and make them all-caps for emphasis.

IT WAS DA BOMB.

I loved it. Jayson did too. For the record, protection was used. This is not a teen pregnancy story.

But I'm getting ahead of myself.

I will say this for Jayson: he did it up right. We went to L20, the super-fine restaurant at the Belden-Stratford Hotel near Lincoln Park. I'm a girl who never dresses up. Not only couldn't I afford nice threads, but when a person has moved as much in their life as I have, you learn to travel light. All my clothes could fit easily in two suitcases.

Remember that fact. It's important later.

Imagine my surprise when the doorbell rang that last afternoon Jayson was in Chicago. I opened it to a white delivery guy in a gray uniform. He held a wrapped box.

"Ronette Bradley?" he asked.

"That's me last time I looked."

"For you."

He handed me the box. I was puzzled but signed for the package and tipped him two bucks. When you clean rooms, you learn that the eleventh commandment is, "Thou Shalt Tip Your Service Person Because, Dammit, They're Getting Paid Doodly." Etch it on a stone tablet.

The box was from Brooklyn Industries, a hip clothing joint on Milwaukee Avenue. It held a black silk dress with red trim that plunged low in both front and back. Also a pair of heels. Red with black trim. Plus a note: "Hot clothes for the hawt girl. C U tonight."

Yes. I melted a little. I melted more when everything fit like it was made for me. My mother actually yelped with happiness when she saw me come out of my room for the date.

"Baby girl, you're in a dress!"

I had to smile. She made it sound like I'd cured cancer.

"Do I look a'ight?" I asked her.

"Baby girl, I'm your mama, so I'd tell you that you looked a'ight if you were wearin' a garbage bag with a duct tape belt. All I can say is that if I was your Jayson, I wouldn't be goin' away to Houseman. I'd be stayin' right here at Northwestern."

I frowned a little. Jayson had been recruited by a bunch

of big schools, including Northwestern University up the road in Evanston. He'd decided on Houseman, mostly because his daddy, James, (not Jim, do not ever call him Jim) had gone there.

But still.

I pushed that thought from my mind. People went to college all the time. It's part of life.

The thought roared back at me in italics.

Yeah, babe. But how many of those people stick with their hometown honey when they go to a place where the girl-to-boy ratio is two-to-one? Don't you know that those college girls are gonna be fightin' over your man?

I told the thought to shut her face. This time, she listened.

The date was a dream. Jayson fetched me in a limo and brought me roses. We talked and laughed all the way downtown. He wore black pants and a black cashmere V-neck sweater with the sleeves pushed up. In the restaurant, we sat next to each other instead of across. When we weren't using our forks and knives, we held hands. We ate seafood bisque, salad with blue cheese dressing, a Kobe beef filet with baby new potatoes and glazed carrots, and hand-cranked mango ice cream for dessert.

We talked more and looked into each other's eyes.

"I'm gonna miss you a lot," Jayson said when the last

dish had been taken away and he'd given his daddy's credit card to the waiter.

"I'm gonna miss you too."

"We gonna text, and Skype, and all that," he promised.

"Works for me," I told him.

He scrunched up his face. "Okay, there's something I gotta say, so I'm just gonna say it."

I had no idea what was coming, but I motioned with my hand for him to bring it.

"I just—I wish you'd gotten the grades to get into Houseman," he declared. "This'd be all different. We could be goin' there together."

I cast my eyes down at the white tablecloth, unable to meet his gaze. I felt a little ashamed at how crappy I'd done in high school. Okay. A lot ashamed.

"I know," I murmured.

"Why, Ronette?" he asked me. "You read more books than anyone. You write great. You even got better SATs than me. Why'd you have to mess up your GPA?"

I shook my head. A lump rose in my throat. "I don't know really. High school just felt like prison."

He cupped his hand under my chin and slowly turned my head. We were looking directly into each other's eyes.

"Do good at CCC," he told me. "Then you can transfer next year."

Next year. That felt like next century. Meanwhile, in twelve hours, he'd be on the way to the Dee Cee.

He signed the credit card slip. We went back to the waiting limo. It was in his arms in that limo that I made the decision. His parents were away for three weeks on Martha's Vineyard. His older sister lived in New York; his big brother worked for a movie company in Los Angeles.

The penthouse would be empty. We'd be alone. I wanted Jayson to know I really loved him. He wanted the same for me.

I called Kalina to tell her I wasn't coming home. She didn't argue.

Let me repeat: it was da bomb. I'm not sorry we did it. It kind of sealed us with him going away and me staying in Chicago.

I stayed overnight. We slept in each other's arms. I was with him in the morning when the cab arrived to take him to O'Hare and drop me at my place. We kissed again and again on my doorstep. I was strong and did not cry. Not even at the last, "I love you."

Not until the cab rolled away. Then, I wept.

Chapter Two

Two weeks later, I was still cleaning rooms. Jayson was in Dee Cee, just about to start classes at the college everyone just called "da House."

I had so many reasons to be low. My job. My school. And my man being seven hundred miles away.

First, work. Here's some free advice from someone who's cleaned thousands of rooms: Never lay down on a hotel bedspread. They barely ever get washed. Don't walk barefoot on a hotel room carpet. The amount of stuff that won't come out of the fibers with a vacuum is wack. Most important, wipe down the TV remote with alcohol before touching it. That woman in the lobby who had a herpes cold sore the size of Ghana could have just been watching Crystal's talk show in your room. I'm just saying.

Next, CCC. I went there to pre-register. What a zoo. And what a dump. No student union, no teams, not even student council. I was all over myself for not figuring out a way to get better grades at Corman.

Finally, Jayson. I knew being apart was going to be hard, but I didn't get how hard. He was doing two-a-day football practices. When he wasn't on the field, he was eating, sleeping, or you-know-whatting. We texted some. Our e-mails were short and calls shorter. That we'd hit it the night before he left only made things worse. Even though it was fun, I wasn't sure that we should do it again for a while. I've seen what happens when hittin' it became the most important thing to a couple. It isn't pretty.

Not that this was a real issue. He was in the Dee Cee, and I was in Chicago. We were geographically challenged.

My mom could tell I was upset. When I saw her in the hotel break room, she gazed at me with concern. She wore a dark blue hotel uniform. She looks a lot like me only with more makeup and her hair is shorter. She's a demoness with cosmetics. I had on my light blue maid's outfit with thick shoes. I learned my first day on the job what happens if you try to scrub a dirty shower in flats. Yuck.

"How you doin', Ronette?" It was just the two of us in a windowless room with candy machines, a coffee pot, harsh lighting, a table, and a few chairs.

"I'm chill."

She peered closely. "You don't look chill. You look like hell."

I shrugged. "Had to scour two ten. You don't want to know why."

"I can imagine." She winced.

I managed a thin smile.

"Did they tip you at least?"

I dug out a folded pamphlet that advertised some weird religion based in Hollywood. "No money. Just this."

Kalina laughed. "That won't get you a sandwich at Subway."

"Or into heaven," I quipped.

I checked my cell. I only had fifteen minutes for break, and there was something I wanted to do before I tackled room 211. There was also the possibility I'd get lucky. There had been a DND—do not disturb sign—hanging on the 211 door before I went on break. DND signs are every maid's bestie. If it was still there when my break was over, I was done for the day. "I gotta go."

"Okay. I'm making spaghetti for dinner. You'll be there?"

I shake my head. "Nah. I got a hot date."

She took me seriously for a second. Then we both cracked up.

"See you later, baby girl."

Two minutes later, I was outside 211. The DND sign was gone. Crap. I had to clean it. I hoped they hadn't checked out unexpectedly. If they were still occupying, all I had to do was make the bed instead of changing the sheets. Then I remembered that they had a dog and cursed the Apex pet policy. It's pet-friendly for the guests but pet-nightmare for the maids. Animals in hotel rooms get bugged out. Bugged out animals shed like crazy. Guess who had to vacuum extra?

Since I wasn't pumped up for a fur fest and had a few more minutes of break, I went back to room 210; the last one I'd cleaned. No one can check in till three, so I entered with my passkey. I had the place to myself. I could even watch Katie or Crystal on TV, if I wanted.

I didn't. I had something better to do. Two somethings, actually.

First, I called Jayson. As usual, I hit his voice mail. Oh well. It was two o'clock in the Dee Cee, which meant he was probably on the football field. I texted him and felt sad all over again. If only I'd studied more …

"Do something about that," I ordered myself.

I had a notebook I took everywhere, even to the hotel. I wrote poems in it. Most of the time, I copied my poems to an el-cheapo laptop I inherited from the hotel lost-and-found. (Word to wise: if you leave something behind in a room, call the hotel office, because they won't contact you out of respect for your privacy.)

I liked to write poetry by hand. Keyboard clicking bugged me. Stupid, I know.

My notebook was on my cleaning cart under a stack of towels. I retrieved it and sat at 210's wooden desk. I found the white Apex Airporter pen I'd replaced forty-five minutes before and thought for a moment about Shaaban Lowe, my favorite writer in the world. He was a poet who told it like it was.

I was ready to tell it like it was. The words came freaky fast.

"The Mirror"

You feelin' so sad
'Cause you think you been had
It makes you feel mad
Opp'site of bein' glad
You look in the mirror
Don't like what'chu see
'Cause the reason that you mad
Starin' right where you be!

There it was. I had it.

In hip-hop, some would call what I wrote "the chorus." I just call it the main part of the poem. Not that any of my teachers ever liked my writing. They said it was too street, too slick, too rap. They wanted me to write like Yeats, Keats, Tennyson, and a bunch of other dead white guys whose stuff put me to sleep. The only one I could stand was Shakespeare, and that's because a lot of his plays have a high body count.

Whatevs. I had the main part of my new poem. Sometimes poetry is a pain. Sometimes it's easy. When it's easy, life is good.

I was ready to tackle 211.

I wish I hadn't. A pool of pungent vomit awaited me on the tile floor outside the bathroom.

I slammed the door and retched. Blech! Then I pulled it together.

"Okay," I told myself. "You're a pro. You got a job to do. Remember what Consuela taught you. Do it."

Consuela was the maid who trained me. She's worked at the Airporter forever, and she's the queen of Windex. My first day, she'd told me that to kill the smell of the really diz-gusting jobs, I should soak foam earplugs in perfume and push them up my nostrils. It would look like a major-league nose pick, but at least I could do what needed to be done.

I was about to raid my cart for earplugs when my cell sounded. I checked caller ID. Dee Cee! It wasn't Jayson's number but I figured it had to be him.

"Hey, baby. I miss you and your guns," I cooed into the phone. I wasn't planning to hit it with him again, but that didn't mean I couldn't flirt.

I heard a throat clear at the other end.

"Ahem. I'm looking for Ms. Ronette Bradley."

Not Jayson. Female. Older. Uh-oh.

I tried to repair the damage. "Yes, this is Ronette Bradley. Yes, I'm sorry, I was expecting my boyfriend and—"

"Hello, Ronette." The woman cut me off. "This is Mrs. Stella Jacobs at the Houseman University Office of Admissions. I know it's late notice, but I suspect that you might not mind when you hear what I have to say. The university would be pleased to offer you a spot in this year's incoming freshman class. Classes start Monday."

Chapter Three

$\mathcal{I}$ screamed.

"Woo-woo-woo-woo-woo-woo-woo-a'ight!"

I pushed Mute on my cell first, though.

I was still flying when I got back to Mrs. Jacobs.

"Ronette, are you still there?" she asked.

"I'm here," I reported.

My heart pounded like crazy. My hand gripped the phone like I was holding a winning Powerball ticket. I saw two lady guests come out of 209 and look at me and shake their heads, because maids are not supposed to be on their phones when on duty. Ha! I wouldn't be a maid for much longer. Jayson, here I come!

Then my celebration ground to a halt. How was I ever going to pay for Houseman?

Mrs. Jacobs answered that question before I could ask it. In part, anyway.

"I am sorry this is such short notice," she said. "But it sometimes happens with those on the waiting list. We are prepared to offer you a fifty percent scholarship of twelve thousand five hundred dollars. The rest of your fees will need to be paid by next Wednesday. Do you understand, Ronette?"

I went for super polite. "Yes, ma'am."

"We're accepting you because of your extraordinary test scores. We're taking a chance and giving you an opportunity. Don't mess it up," she warned.

I calmed myself enough to ask the obvious questions. "How do I get to Washington? What classes do I take? Where am I going to live?"

"How you get here is your business," Mrs. Jacobs declared severely. I pictured her as a pinched lady with her hair in a bun. "The rest will be in an e-mail from the admissions office. I have other calls to make, Ronette. Congratulations. I hope you decide to join us. Let me be the first to welcome you to Houseman."

She clicked off.

I stood there in shock. Then, I did two things.

First, I screamed again. Longer, louder, and happier.

Then, I called Jayson, expecting to get his voice mail,

which I did. I left the most wack message in the history of wack messages.

"Jayson, it's me, it's me. Omigod, you're not going to believe it. They just called me. I mean Houseman, and they're taking me, they're taking me. Can you believe it? They accepted me from the wait-list, and they're giving me a scholarship. Not the whole thing but half. And I don't know how I'm coming to Washington or even if I can come, but if there's a way for me to come, you know I'm coming. Omigod. Omigod. Omigod. I got into Houseman. Call meeeeeee!"

Then I clicked off, texted him, "Ck yr VM now!!!!" and pushed my maid service cart to one side of the corridor.

Next stop, my mother.

I ran all the way to the front desk.

Kalina was alone, getting caught up on paperwork. The lobby was quiet. Soft piano music played on the sound system; a couple of Latino janitors mopped the tile floor. I dashed past them at full speed and skidded to a stop in front of her.

"Mama! Mama! You won't believe what just happened!"

My mom looked up and grinned at my excitement. "You found ten grand in cash?"

"Better!" I exclaimed.

She raised her eyebrows. "Better than ten grand? Then you better tell me."

I took a deep breath. I wanted this moment to have an impact.

"I just got a call from the admissions office at Houseman. They accepted me. Classes start on Monday."

Here are the emotions that painted my mother's face, one after another:

Joy.

Shock.

Concern.

Surprise.

Disbelief.

Worry.

Pride.

And finally, joy again.

"Oh, baby girl. … "

She reached her arms over the counter for a hug. I hugged her back. We held it a long time. I realized then and there that if I went away to Houseman, my mother would be alone for the first time since she got pregnant with me as a teenager. What would that be like for her?

What would that be like for me?

"Tell me everything," she ordered when the hug was over. "Word for word."

I did, right down to the twelve-five scholarship. "I need to come up with the other half."

I didn't say so, but I was now big-time worried about the money. Like so many folks, we lived paycheck to paycheck. I knew there were grants and loans for kids who wanted to go to an expensive college, but no way could I be approved for that over the weekend. You have to jump through a lot of hoops.

My mother took my hand. "Baby girl, you don't worry none about the money."

"What do you mean?"

She gave me a squeeze. "What I mean is that your mama has something socked away for a rainy day. It could take me a day or two to get it, but that tuition will get paid." She grinned. "Bet you're loving your mama right now, huh, baby girl?"

I loved my mama all the time. She was honest, true, and devoted. I never knew who my dad was. Didn't care. Kalina had gotten pregnant when she was seventeen, and the guy took off. She'd never chased him because she didn't want to have to deal with him. I couldn't blame her. Any brother who'd run like that was a brother you should run from. He was scum.

Her co-host at the front desk, a young white woman from Texas named Alexis, came out from the back. She had a toothy grin, blonde hair in a high ponytail, and the thickest Texas drawl and craziest expressions I'd ever heard. I liked her. When my mom told her about me and college, she hugged me too.

"Kalina and Ronette, I'm happier 'n a gopher in soft dirt for y'all! Why don't y'all go to the Starbucks and get some coffee and cake to celebrate?" she asked. "My treat!"

She pressed a twenty into my mom's hands. I thanked her big-time. Like I said, she was a nice lady.

The hotel had a Starbucks. In the morning, the line took forever. Since we maids put Starbucks packets in the room by the coffeemakers, the line always struck me as craziness. In the afternoon, it was quiet. I ordered a whipped-creamy drink. My mom got a giant Americano. We found a table where we could see the front desk. If a rush of early check-ins arrived, my mom would have to leave.

If I thought this celebration was going to be a gush-about-wonderful-Ronette fest, I was wrong. My mother turned all serious.

"Ronette, I don't want you to worry about the details of going to college," she said softly. "We will get you to Washington, and get you to wherever you're going to live, and get school paid for. What I want you to worry about is doing good in your classes."

I licked a little whipped cream from my lips. "I know. I gotta do good this time."

"You don't have much experience with doin' good in school," Kalina observed. "How you plannin' to change that? Believe me, baby girl, I'm not payin' for you to go to college to bump uglies wit' your boyfriend, and then find you back here cleaning rooms after you flunk out!"

I tensed. "I'm gonna do better, Mama."

She shook her index finger at me. "How? 'Zactly how? I've been hearin' the same damn thing since sixth grade." She imitated one of the many teachers who had lamented to her in the parent-teacher conferences she never missed. " 'We're sorry, Ms. Bradley, but your Ronette? Well, we just don't understand it. She's just not working up to her full potential.' "

My mom had me nailed. I barely studied in middle school or high school. Biology labs were stupid. History textbooks were boring. I'd always rather just go to the library or read online. That's how my head got filled up with the random facts and vocabulary words that helped me on the SATs but didn't help my GPA. I knew that Haile Selassie had been emperor of Ethiopia, and that Adamou Ide was the national poet of Niger. That Audie Murphy was the most famous American soldier of the Second World War. Everyone knows that Jackie Robinson was the first black ballplayer in the major leagues, but I knew that Larry Doby was the second, and Satchel Paige was the seventh. I could tell you the names of all seven original Mercury astronauts, how the AIDS virus was isolated, and who was president between Harding and Hoover. What I couldn't do was pass a social studies test on how a bill becomes law.

As my mom talked, I had a vision of myself in four months, doing just what she predicted. I was back in my maid's uniform, cleaning up barf.

No way.

"I don't know how I'll do it," I said. "I'll just do better! I won't let you down."

Her finger didn't stop wagging. "You better do better. An' you better figure out how. 'Cause I will bet on you blind for one semester. That's all," she promised.

"I won't let you down," I repeated.

She rubbed her chin, and then took another sip of her drink. "I hope not, baby girl. I hope not."

I hoped not too.

Chapter Four

It turned out that Alexis—bless her!—had about a million frequent flyer miles. When my mom told her that I needed to get to Washington, she bought me a ticket. I told her I owed her one. She just said to make my mother proud.

The flight from Chicago to Dee Cee is two hours. I was supposed to touch down at three in the afternoon. But when three o'clock came, I was still at Gate 46 at O'Hare while mechanics worked on my plane's landing gear. Finally, they rolled the 757 away and brought in another plane. Then, a thunderstorm moved in, and they closed the airport. I didn't get off the ground until seven, which meant I wouldn't land until nine, which meant I'd be lucky to make it to Houseman by ten. I was tired, cranky, and hungry. Airport food tastes like straw.

The approach to Dee Cee made me feel better, though. I pressed my face against the window as we descended. It was easy to pick out the Capitol and the Washington Monument. Then I spotted the Jefferson Memorial on the shore of the Potomac. And the White House. Seeing it made me think of President Obama; I automatically ran the names of the presidents through my head. Backward. By the time I reached Andrew Jackson, we were on final approach.

I texted Jayson the moment the tires touched the runway, "Here!"

He texted back, "Mt me bge claim."

I was here. I was really here. I was really going to Houseman.

I could not mess this up.

It was a dream walk to baggage claim. I had two bags waiting for me—everything I owned. I wore jeans, a black tank top, Keds sneakers, and carried a backpack with my wallet, poetry notebook, and laptop. Just before baggage claim, I went through a revolving security door and past two African American TSA ladies looking bored to death. I started to tell myself that if I didn't get decent grades, those guards could be me someday.

Then I shut up. There he was.

Jayson.

Damn. Two-a-day practices had been good to him. He was even more buff than when he'd left Chicago. He wore black shorts. And—wow—a sleeveless Houseman football practice shirt. His bronzed guns gleamed at me.

Without knowing how I got there, I was in his arms crying happy tears. "I can't … can't believe I'm here!"

"I can," he quipped. "Come on, let's get your stuff. Oh! Wait. I brought you something."

There was a yellow plastic bag at his feet that I hadn't even noticed. He gave it to me. "Thought you might be wantin' this."

When I saw what was inside, I kissed him. It was a black-and-silver Houseman University T-shirt, long-sleeve girls' style. I pulled it over my tank top. Baggy, but good enough. Jason took out his iPhone and snapped a pic. A moment later, he posted it to Blackplanet. I was official.

A'ight.

There's a Metro station at National Airport and another in Adams-Morgan, the Dee Cee neighborhood where Houseman is located. Jayson said it was the fastest way to campus. We had to hustle because he had a football team bed check at ten thirty. The whole trip took about thirty minutes. I rode the entire way with my head on his shoulder and his arm around me. It was incredible to be back with my man.

We grabbed a cab outside the Adams-Morgan station. Jayson said if I didn't have my suitcases, we could easily walk the fifteen minutes to "da House." From the cab, I could see that the hood was hopping on a Friday night. Kids of all ages and colors swarmed restaurants, bars, and nightclubs. It was as busy as the South Side.

"This is where the action is," Jayson declared.

"It's fantastic," I breathed. There were so many college kids. I was one of them now.

I told myself yet again not to mess this up.

"I'll take you everywhere," he promised. "All the good clubs, all the hot joints. This place'll be home before you know it."

We got to Houseman. The campus was at the top of a small hill and had an actual gate. Jayson told the driver to go to the admin building. He gave me a quick tour on the way, though it was night and I couldn't make out much. Dorm names passed in a whir. Ditto classroom buildings, labs, the library, the chapel, the quad that Jayson said was the center of "da House," and then finally the admin building where the housing office was open till midnight to take care of late-arriving students like me.

The cab dropped us outside the brick building. We left my bags with the guard and headed to housing on the second floor. The person on duty was a student, a senior guy with unfortunate skin. I thought for a second how cool it was that he was black until I reminded myself that this was a black school.

"Um, so, let's see …" The guy leafed through a purple binder, looking for my name. It took him a while. In fact, he didn't find me until he checked the very last page.

"Ronette Bradley! Here you are. McMaster dorm, third floor, room three thirteen. A quad. Let me get you a key and a school ID. You'll need to show this to dorm security."

Jayson punched the air. "She's in McMaster?"

The guy nodded. "Lucky, I know."

"What's McMaster?" I was clue free.

"Just the best dorm here," Jayson chortled. "Built two years ago, high speed everything, dining room downstairs, right in the middle of campus. The quads have two bedrooms, a living room, and a kitchen. Girl, you lucked out!"

I grinned wildly as the zitty guy gave me my keycard. I signed a few forms, and that was that. I wanted to get to my room and settle in. Maybe I'd even meet my roommates. As Jayson and I picked up my bags from the guard downstairs, I realized I'd forgotten to get their names. No biggie. I'd find out soon enough. I just hoped they weren't party hearty types.

Jayson helped me with my stuff across campus, then stopped at the entrance to McMaster. It was a huge dorm, all white with four floors. "Hate to do this to you, but it's ten twenty-one and bed check is in nine minutes. I'm gonna have to run. Literally. Don't worry. There's an elevator."

I snaked my arms around his neck. "Even if I recite the alphabet backward? In Swahili?"

"That might get me hot. Start."

"Ze, ye, we, ve—"

I got no further before he kissed me. Quickly. Then he took off.

"Eight minutes!" he called over his shoulder.

I laughed and hoisted my suitcases. After I flashed my new ID to the guard, I found the elevator and took it to the third floor. I was greeted by deep, pounding music. I followed the music down the hall. Crap and a half. It was coming out of 313.

I put down my suitcases and opened the door.

Damn. I walked into a roaring college dorm room party. Room filled with kids. Music wailing. Dancing, shouting, clapping, sweating.

A second later, I stepped out to reassess. This was my room? Sweet Jesus, please help—

Suddenly, the door opened. An imposing girl stepped out. She was taller than Jayson and didn't look happy.

"Who are you?" she demanded, eyeing my bags with suspicion.

"I'm Ronette Bradley," I said, standing my ground.

"Why you here? We didn't invite you."

That got my back up. No one talks to me like that, male or female. I don't care whether they can dunk a basketball without jumping.

"I'm here because this is my room. Housing sent me here." I flashed my keycard and one of the forms that I'd gotten at the housing office.

The girl laughed and softened. "Funny. I'm Arica Adams, this is my quad, and it's full. You better go back to housing."

"That's … that's crazy!" I sputtered.

Arica shook her head, not unkind. "Nah. It's Houseman. Go back and tell them they put you in the wrong room. Know what? After they get you settled? Come back. I'll intro you around. You seem a'ight."

"But—"

"Later, Ronette."

The door closed. The pounding music got even louder. I was stuck. This was not my room, at least not for tonight.

Welcome to Houseman.

Chapter Five

A girl hasn't really lived till she's spent her first night at college sleeping in a racquetball court. That girl was me. Here's how it went down.

The nice guard in McMaster—an older man named Mr. Newlan—took pity on me when I said I had to go back to housing. He called someone from campus security to drive me and told the officer to stick with me until I got wherever I was going for the evening. I could have kissed him for that. My shoulders ached from dragging around my suitcases; my backpack dug into my shoulder blades.

The officer, whose name was Sharma, was in her fifties and the mother of a Houseman senior she said was the editor of school literary magazine. That perked me up a little; I wondered if the magazine published stuff like I wrote. Then there was no more time to wonder because I was back with the zitty guy in the housing office. He gushed apologies and told me to tell Sharma to take me to temp housing.

"Come back tomorrow, we'll get this worked out," he promised.

"What's temp housing?" I asked suspiciously.

"Don't worry, you'll be fine," was his response.

"What is it?" I pressed.

"You'll be fine," he repeated. Then his cell chimed, which cut off any chance for me to press for more details.

I went back down to Sharma's car and reported what the zitty senior had told me.

"Ah, the gym," she told me.

I yelped despite the fact that I was bone-tired after this long day. "The what?"

"Don't worry, you'll be fine," she said as she started up the cruiser.

Word to wise: When a bunch of people all tell you, "Don't worry, you'll be fine?" Worry.

It turned out that the Houseman athletic facility had six racquetball courts in addition to the usual basketball courts, swimming pool, weight room, and a full field house. Those courts were being used as temporary housing for kids whom the housing office had somehow failed, until they could get squared away. For instance, me.

My new home was court five. I kid you not.

I let myself into the all-white court with the red lines on the walls. I'd never played racquetball. Right then and there, I vowed I never would. I did settle down on one of the four cots; the other three were empty. I stowed my luggage, found a bathroom, and washed off the day's grime. Then I staggered back and turned off the lights. The windowless room plunged into blackness. I had to crawl on hands and knees to where I thought my bed might be. Luckily, I only bashed the frame with my shoulder instead of my forehead.

Then came a text from Kalina. "How are you?"

I thought of a bunch of ace responses.

In prison.

In Russia.

Cn u maybe gt me a rm at Apex DC?

I sent none of these. I just texted back, "Here. Alive. Sleeping."

I closed my eyes but I couldn't sleep, so I imagined roaring jets.

An energetic girl's voice woke me.

"Good morning, good morning, Ronette! Got coffee,

got juice, got doughnuts, got whatever it takes to get you goin', so get yourself up. Let's get goin'! Big day ahead! New digs, new roommate, and lunch with me!"

I opened my eyes and rubbed them blearily. A petite girl with wild dark curls, snapping dark eyes, a great smile, and a dangerously tight red dress stood over me. She held a foam cup in one hand and a chocolate doughnut in the other.

"Well, here we go!" she exclaimed with a laugh. "Ronette Bradley is officially awake! Rise and shine! It's eleven thirty in the morning, sleepy head. Big day ahead! Big day!"

My future husband should take notice. I am not what would be called a morning person. That was one of my big problems in middle school and high school. I wasn't even awake until the school day was half over. It's hard to muster interest in dissecting a flatworm when you're yawning at it.

"Who are you?" I croaked.

"I'm Marta. I got to school late because of a family emergency, and I'm telling you to drink this coffee. That's a direct order."

She pushed the cup in my direction. Normally I don't like being told what to do, but I was in a weakened state. Besides, I liked this girl. Her energy rocked. I took the cup and sipped. Good. Not too hot either. I drained half of it in one big gulp.

"Outstanding, soldier," she told me. "Now a bite of doughnut and we'll be ready to roll. I've already checked in at housing. They're supposed to have us squared away by three o'clock. Get it together. We can eat lunch in Adams-Morgan and still get to housing by fourteen thirty. Rise and shine!"

This girl sounded like a drill sergeant, so it was hard to disobey her. I ate the doughnut and drank more coffee. Dammit if I didn't feel better. When she told me where to find a shower, and that she'd meet me in front of the gym in thirty minutes for our trip to Adams-Morgan, I did that too.

I was a little slow getting out the door. Marta wasn't happy.

"You're late," she declared as I stepped into the warm September sunshine.

"Just five minutes!" I protested, taking in my first daylight look at this part of the Houseman campus. It was leafy and green. Off in the distance were tennis courts, a baseball field, and a hill with a water tower atop it.

"If we're going to be friends—and we're going to be friends—you need to be on time. I won't make you wait; you don't make me wait. Dealy? Oh! There's the shuttle. Let's run!"

Marta pointed to a van that had just pulled up in front of the building. We hustled over and climbed on. It turned out to be the free shuttle that took kids around the campus as well as to Adams-Morgan.

"How'd you even know about this van?" I asked her when we'd found seats in the back. We were the only two people riding. Marta still wore her red dress. I had on clean jeans and the Houseman shirt that Jayson had brought me. Even after the housing disaster, I wanted people to know I was a Houseman sister.

Marta smiled knowingly. "I'm very smart."

Thinking about my shirt made me think about Jayson. I dug out my phone, which I'd wisely silenced so I could sleep. There were a bunch of texts from him, including one that said he'd be at football practice till four but wanted to get together after that. I texted him back how that would be fine.

"Who you texting?" Marta asked.

"Boyfriend."

Marta laughed. "Boyfriend? You just got here! Oh! You mean your boyfriend back home. That won't last."

I bristled a little. "It will too last. He's right here at Houseman."

Her eyes grew wide. "Really? Omigod, you are so lucky. Tell me all about him."

As the van rolled into Adams-Morgan, I told her about Jayson and me and how I came to be admitted to Houseman so late.

"What about you?" I asked, noticing that Marta was watching the street carefully.

"Boyfriend-free. Lots of comp at this school. Don't have my hopes up." She signaled the driver that he should pull over at the next stop. "You ever eat Ethiopian?"

I never had. But soon I was an Ethiopian food fanatic.

We ended up at a busy place called Addis, which I knew from random reading was named for Addis Ababa, the capital of Ethiopia. There were plenty of wooden tables on a terrace that faced busy Eighteenth Street NW. Marta explained that if we walked south for a half hour, we'd end up near the White House.

She ordered. There were no knives or forks. Instead, you tore off a piece of this sticky, flexible flatbread called *injira*, and used it to pick up cooked veggies, chicken, egg, lentils, and whatnot. It sounds messy and it is, a little. But it was soooo good. After yesterday's not-so-fine dining at O'Hare, I was crazy hungry.

"How do you know about this food?"

She swallowed a mouthful of *injira* and *kik alicha*, a sort of split pea stew. "My dad's in AFRICOM, so we lived overseas. I've been there. Ethiopia, I mean."

"Your dad's in what?"

"AFRICOM. African Central Command. U.S. Army," she said. "I'm a brat. I've lived everywhere. Germany, England, New Jersey, California, Japan, you name it. Ask me where home is."

Ah. So she was an army brat. That's what other people call kids whose parents are in the military. I'd read about them. They tend to grow up all over, as their parents get moved from base to base.

I took the bait anyway. "Where's home?"

Marta shrugged. "Don't know. Kinda weird when you're Cuban like me."

"What?" I scoffed. "You're black!"

"Skin maybe. *Pero mis padres son de Cuba. Es por eso que yo soy cubana.*"

I grinned. She'd said that her parents were from Cuba, and because of that she considered herself Cuban. I knew I was about to rock her world.

"*Qué bueno. Yo tengo solamente una madre. Yo soy de Chicago. Y yo he vivido muchos lugares también.*"

There are real advantages to working with a lot of Latina ladies. I had said, in decent Spanish, "That's great. I only have a mother. I'm from Chicago. I've lived a lot of places too."

She stared at me. "Okay, Ronette. I'm impressed. Open wide."

She indicated my mouth.

I did as I was told. She tore off some *injira*, wrapped a huge piece of chicken in it, and popped it between my lips. "That's called *goorsha* in Amharic," she explained.

I chewed and then swallowed. "The language of Ethiopia, right?"

"Right! *Goorsha* is an act of friendship. The bigger the piece, the bigger the friendship."

I pointed to her mouth. She opened it. I put in an equally big chunk of *injira* and chicken.

"*Goorsha*," I told her.

I had just made my first Houseman friend. After a rocky start, things were looking up.

Chapter Six

"I hope this goes better than last night," I told Jayson.

"From what you said, it can't go any worse," he reassured me.

"Just do it," Marta urged.

The three of us stood in front of room 444 in McMaster. I held the keycard in my hard. Supposedly, my new roommate was a girl from New York named Lori Williams.

After a long lunch, Marta and I had stopped in at housing. We'd tried to lobby the woman on duty to put us in a room together. No luck. Marta was assigned into a triple in Hughes, while I got sent here. I helped Marta move into her room first. Her roommates seemed okay. There was a hugely overweight sister from Los Angeles, and a girl from Mississippi who played cymbals in the

Houseman marching band. I hoped she didn't plan to practice in the room.

Once we got Marta settled, we met up with Jayson. They liked each other immediately, which was good because it sucks when your boyfriend and a new friend don't get along. We walked to McMaster together. Marta and I carried one of my suitcases, Jayson the other one. I was grateful for their moral support in case I ran into another disaster.

That's exactly what happened. It just took longer to unfold.

I put my keycard in the door. The indicator turned green, like the locks on the rooms at the Apex Airporter. I sincerely hoped I would not be greeted with a pool of throw-up or an off-the-hook college party.

No vomit. No party. Instead, I walked into an incredibly well-equipped dorm room; more like someone's actual bedroom than a place to sleep while away at college.

"Wow," Marta breathed as she took it in.

"No kidding," Jayson agreed. "This Lori chick got herself some chip."

I looked around. I'd vacuumed enough carpets to know this rug did not come from Target. It was thick wool with an intricate pattern, like something hand-woven in Tunisia or Yemen. The desk was not dorm-issue. It was gorgeous black African teak. There were two beds. One was a regular dorm cot—plain frame and thin mattress. The other was oversized and four poster, with a plush pink bedspread and lush pillows. Guess which one was Lori's.

The art on the walls was all framed hip-hop posters, signed by the performers.

"Who is this girl?" Marta asked.

I didn't know. I checked the bathroom—we were lucky enough in McMaster to have our own sink and toilet, though the showers were down the hall. Lori had mounted a gorgeous storage unit on the back of the door. I opened it cautiously; I couldn't help myself. It held an assortment of high-end cosmetics, perfumes, brushes, clips, and combs that my mother would have coveted. She'd also attached a snazzy makeup mirror above the sink.

We were such a toiletries mismatch. My own bathroom stuff fit into a pink case I bought at the Dollar Store.

"Um, Ronette?" Marta called to me. "You need to see this."

I came back into the main room. Marta had opened the clothes closet and was pointing into it. My jaw fell. I'd never seen so many designer clothes in my life. And the shoes! Dozens of pairs. I am not a shoe person, but I can read labels. Brian Atwood. Jimmy Choo. Christian Louboutin. On and on and on.

Damn. The shoes alone were worth more than my mom's annual income.

"BAP," Jayson said confidently.

"Maybe," I agreed.

"BAP?" Marta asked.

"She's an army brat, forgive her ignorance," I told Jayson. "Marta, it means Black American Princess," I explained. "Grew up rich. Richie-rich tastes. Daddy's credit card, drives a BMW, never worked a day in her life."

"Hey now," Jayson cautioned. "I have Daddy's credit card."

"You use it wisely," I told him.

"What about the posters? What's up with that?" Marta asked.

I shrugged. "Maybe she needs to rebel against Mommy and Daddy."

"I think we better get you unpacked," Jayson suggested.

It took all of fifteen minutes to unpack me. Like I said, I'd packed light. Lori had put up some sort of thick fabric divider between her four-fifths of the closet and her roommate-to-be's one-fifth so the dirt on her roommate's clothes wouldn't touch her precious Marni dresses. I was surprised she didn't have it booby trapped.

My shoes went under my bed with my suitcases. There was no hope for them on the closet floor.

I can say this: I hadn't met Lori Williams, but she hadn't made a good first impression. In fact, without ever speaking a word to her, I kind of despised her. I figured she was the kind of person who would never stay at the Apex because that would be slummin'. If she did stay there, there's no way she'd leave the maid a tip. Not even after she barfed up Champagne onto the bathroom floor.

An hour later, Marta had gone back to her dorm while Jayson and I were out together on what everyone called the quad. It was a monster grassy area at the center of campus about the size of eight football fields. There was a flagpole in the center and giant cherry and maple trees along the sides that separated the quad from classroom buildings. At the south end of the quad was the big school library. At the north end, the admin building. The quad was Houseman's center of gravity. If it was on the periodic table of elements, it would be in the middle with the symbol Qu.

Even though classes hadn't started, the quad was rockin'. We found a spot under the trees where I could take in the crowd. There were kids laughing, playing music, dancing and popping, and throwing footballs around. I smelled barbecued chicken and pork ribs cooking on grills. There were all different groups. The athletes seemed to be hanging together, as did various clusters of girls. Some were dressed up, others dressed down. There were a bunch of goth-looking kids who looked like they'd stepped out of a suburban white high school. I even saw kids in Houseman LBGTQ Alliance T-shirts.

"What do you think?" Jayson asked.

"I think it's amazing." This was college the way I dreamed of it.

"You ready for registration tomorrow?"

"Ready as I'll ever be," I told him. I had brought my poetry notebook out to the quad with me in the vague hope that I'd be able to do some writing. I snuck a peek at it. Maybe all these kids around me would be inspiring.

Jayson must have seen my glance. "I know that face," he joke-accused. "How about I give you some space so you can scribble to your heart's content?"

I raised my eyebrows at him. "Scribble?"

"Excuse me. Add to the supply of the world's great black American literature."

I laughed. "That's better. What's up for tonight?"

"I'm working on something. I'll text you."

He leaned in and kissed me. I kissed him back. The kiss went on long enough to leave me breathless and wondering if my don't-hit-it policy was truly in my own self-interest. But where would we even go if we decided to do it? Dorm rooms weren't private. That left outdoors, cars, and the like. Gross.

I realized we still had to talk about the whole hittin' it thing. We hadn't really had a convo about it. Things had been pretty hectic. I considered bringing it up right then and there, but I wasn't sure what to say. Plus, I really, really wanted to write.

That's what I did after Jayson went to hang with the football players. I opened my notebook and started again on what I'd worked on in room 210 at the Apex just two days before. Just two days! Everything had changed.

> You feelin' so sad
> 'Cause you think you been had
> It makes you feel mad
> Opp'site of bein' glad
> You look in the mirror
> Don't like what'chu see
> 'Cause the reason that you mad
> Starin' right where you be!
>
> It change in a instant
> It change on a dime
> Your phone be ringing

"Honey here's a good time
To get your ass outta town to a place
You wanna be
Not New York, not LA, but just
The Dee Cee!"

Here the thing, though
You could be fraudulent, whoa!
With your shirt wit' the logo
And the name that gives you fame
But when push comes to shove
And the Bard says, "There's the rub,"
What the grade you gonna get
When the answers all be set
And the girl in the mirror
Don't like what she see
'Cause the reason she be mad
Starin' right where she be!

It was flowing, and the words that I was writing were the ones that I wanted to say. Everything was coming together. I was in the zone.

I stayed in that zone for hours. I wrote for so long that I didn't realize the sun had gone down, the quad had cleared out, my stomach was rumbling with hunger, and I had goose bumps on my arms from not bringing a sweatshirt.

What got me out of the zone was a text from Jayson.

Short, simple, and to the point: "Yo! Where u b? U rdy to gt down in da house?"

Chapter Seven

Everybody say hey, ho! Hey, ho! Everybody say hey, ho! Hey, ho!"

Some rapper's voice pounded through the excellent sound system in the basement of the three-story house on Kalorama Road NW. The room was jammed with Houseman kids, mostly dressed to thrill. It was hot, sweaty, raw, intense—exactly the kind of scene I went out of my way to avoid back in Chicago. A girl could lose control, and then where would she be in an hour? Upstairs in a bedroom doing something that she would regret in the morning?

But I wasn't in Chicago anymore. Plus, I'd already done that thing she'd regret in the morning, and I didn't regret it. It had been with the guy I loved, and it had been great. That I wasn't necessarily ready to repeat it did not mean I was sorry. That guy was in the basement with me and my new bestie, Marta. We were in the midst of the crowd, flinging our arms overhead with each, "Hey, ho!"

It was three hours later. Jayson, Marta, and I had eaten a late dinner in the McMaster dining room (Mexican night, fajitas and tacos, passable). Then we dressed and Jayson called a cab to take us to this party. It was in a house in Adams-Morgan owned by a Houseman fraternity. Because it was off-campus, the usual rules against alcohol didn't apply. Off-campus parties were big at both Houseman and Howard University, the other HBCU in the Dee Cee.

Jayson wore black pants, a black vest, a white shirt with a narrow collar, and a skinny tie. He looked fine. Marta had on a dress even tighter than the red one she'd worn earlier; this one was zebra-striped. Me? I could have worn the dress Jayson had bought me for our date in Chicago, but I decided to dress down in jeans and a simple-patterned shirt. Bad idea. I had the worst look in the room.

It didn't matter much, though. All that mattered in the basement was the music, the dancing, the heat, the rawness, and the bodies. I'm not the best dancer. I sure can't pop like Mister Wiggles. But I still had fun.

That changed when we took a break and went upstairs.

The upstairs was a hive of rooms full of students laughing, partying, and having a big ol' time. That was good. What wasn't good was how my boyfriend got mobbed by fly babes the minute we'd closed the basement door.

"Oh, Jayson! What classes are you taking?"

A light-skinned tall girl with a model's body and a face like a young Halle Berry ran over, pushing Marta and me away like a couple of orange plastic traffic cones. Then Halle Berry Junior had to make room for three more girls with bodies of death and chests that made mine seem concave.

"Jayson! We're so excited to watch your first game!"

"Oh, Jayson! Is coach gonna start you?

"Jayson, Jayson! There's a party at the Kappa house on Thursday night! Will you come and bring some friends?"

These three wore ass-hugger skirts that were short, shorter, and shortest. Jayson introduced them as Shaneen, Marie, and Zenobia. He said they were cheerleaders. To me, they were the three heads of a Chimera from a Greek myth. When I say Greek, I don't mean fraternities and sororities either. I mean the real thing.

I'll say this for Jayson: my man did it right. He introduced me as his girlfriend. Not that it mattered.

The cheerleaders and junior Halle didn't make nice. In fact, they didn't say anything that wasn't directed at my boyfriend.

"Jayson, you look so fine tonight!"

"You gonna hang wit' us later?"

"What frat you gonna pledge?"

"We'll see you at the party after the game!"

Jayson didn't lead them on, but he didn't tell them to jump in the Potomac either. Meanwhile, I hoped I didn't look as insecure as I felt. As the pack prattled on, I reminded myself that I was way better off here at Houseman with Jayson than back in Chicago without him.

Thankfully, the girls moved on, all kiss-kiss and wiggling butts. A bunch of buff guys replaced them. One was the quarterback, another a linebacker, the third the team kicker. I didn't catch their names, so I thought of them as QB, LB, and K. They were polite to Marta and me. The talk was again aimed at my man, though with a different purpose.

"You thinkin' about joining this frat?" QB asked.

"Mebbe," Jayson allowed.

"You need to check 'em all out," LB advised.

"You gotta join someplace," QB said.

"I'm not joining a frat," K confided to Marta.

"That's 'cause he a loser," LB said.

"Hey, man, I kick balls, stay off my case," K fired back.

We all laughed. Then K—whose name turned out to be Kevyn, so K wasn't a bad nickname—asked Marta if she wanted to dance. Marta said okay. The other football players went to the basement with them. At last, Jayson and I were alone.

"You're a popular boy," I observed. I was still reeling from the Attack of the Short Skirts.

"Ain't no girl in this room but you," he declared.

Okay. Major awwww moment there.

I smiled. "You prep that line?"

"Coach told us to use it. Go ask the guys, they'll say so."

This time I laughed. It was impossible to be down around him.

"What's all this about joining a frat?" I asked.

"They're big at Houseman. Huge, actually. Come here. I wanna show you something."

He took me by the arm and led me through the noisy crowd until we reached a quiet back room. He flicked on the light. It was filled with trophies, awards, and photographs of leaders and performers from around the country and the world. I recognized many faces from my online reading. All men.

"All members of this frat," he told me. "There are five others here at Houseman. You get into a frat like this, you're kinda set for life. It ain't just what you know, it's who you know. Your frat brothers are like real brothers. Except you got ten thousand of 'em around the world from all the other black schools. Sororities same thing. You oughta think about pledging."

I thought about the cheerleaders. They had to be in a sorority. I didn't need to be in an all-girls club. This was a black college. Did we need to self-segregate by sex?

"No thanks."

Jayson was unfazed. "No prob. You can change your mind. Rush doesn't start until January. You'll see. Come on, let's go back downstairs."

He took me by the arm; I loved him escorting me through that crowd. We got lots of looks even though I was horribly underdressed. I figured peeps were thinking: *Who's that girl with Jayson Jones?*

Downstairs, the recorded hip-hop had stopped. Instead, a girl with hair to her ass, a body as hot as the cheer-leaders', a black sleeveless dress with thigh-high boots, and skin the color of creamy coffee, was rapping to a big crowd who cheered her on:

> *You make me put you through hell*
> *You really truly smell*
> *You put the F in fart*

I hate you with all my heart
You're poison that Poison Control
Ought to put with mayo on a roll!

Ouch. She was so bad that I winced.

The crowd seemed to eat it up, though, laughing and cheering her on.

"You know who that is, right?" Jayson asked me.

"The world's worst rapper?"

He laughed. "Nah. That's Chyna. She's a freshman too."

Chyna, Chyna …

I tried to place the name. Jayson had said it like it was someone I should know. Then I had it.

"Chyna, the talk show host's daughter? Crystal's daughter?"

"The one," Jayson confirmed.

I didn't watch much TV, but even I knew Crystal. If you were American and had a pulse, you knew her. She had the most popular afternoon talk show on TV, syndicated across the country and around the world. From poor beginnings in Memphis, Tennessee, she'd become a local news reporter, then a local news anchor, and then a talk show host. Now she had her top-rated show, a magazine named after her, a movie production company, and a ranking as one of the most powerful women in the world. My mother was hooked on Crystal. She'd DVR her show during the day and watch it when she came home at night. She saved the really good ones for rewatching.

Chyna was Crystal's party-girl daughter. I'd read about her. She was going to Houseman?

"What sorority is she gonna join?" I asked dryly as Chyna finished her rap—if you could call it that!—to big-time hollering.

Marta came over to join us.

"That's Chyna!" she said excitedly.

"So I heard. What'd you think?" I asked.

"I think she's gorgeous! I watch her mom's show every day. Or used to, anyway. It was on Armed Forces Television. Did you know she OD'd when she was in high school?" Marta asked.

"The mother?"

"Not Crystal, Chyna! She's been in rehab like five times."

"Well, she may be good at rehab," I said with a sniff. "But she can't rap worth—"

"Oh? And you can?"

I turned around. Chyna was standing there, hands on hips. She glared at me. "Who are you?"

Look. I'm not an idiot. I'd just said something mean

about her behind the girl's back. That was catty, and not how my mama had raised me. I needed to say sorry, and I needed to feel sorry. Even if Chyna couldn't write a poem if her life depended on it.

"I'm so sor—"

"Know what? I don't care who you are! Get out of my face and don't get there again. Don't you know who I am? You better pray you don't go to Houseman because you do not want me as your enemy!" She stomped away.

Jayson, Marta, and I looked at each other. I'd just managed to piss off the most famous freshman girl at Houseman. Suddenly, I wanted to get back to my dorm room as quickly as I could. Marta offered to walk me home. Jayson decided to stay and hang with his football buds some more. I said that was fine.

I was in my bed thirty minutes later. My roommate, Lori, wasn't there. I'd have to wait till morning to meet her. But I wasn't thinking about that. What I was thinking was this: Hotel maids knew how to mind their mouths. Why hadn't I minded mine?

Chapter Eight

The next morning—Sunday—I finally met Lori.

I'd set my alarm since registration and book buying was at two. I'd already set up my classes by computer, but there were always last minute changes.

There was one thing I was really excited about. I hadn't really understood until I registered how different college is from high school. College classes met just two or three times a week for eighty minutes or an hour each time. Other than that, my time would be my own. Best of all, I did not have to take any early morning classes unless I wanted them.

I woke up early so I'd have time to shower, eat, and get ready. I was gonna meet Jayson on the quad around noon, and then we'd go to the field house together. What I forgot to do was put my cell phone under my pillow so the alarm would only wake me. My alarm tone is annoying on purpose. It's the 1990s girl group the Spice Girls singing "Wannabe," maybe the worst song in the history of bad songs. I chose it because I hate it so much I'd never sleep through it. To make super sure I wake up, the volume is cranked.

Posh Spice had just finished singing about what she really, really wants, and I was still clawing my way back from sleep to reality, when a female voice I didn't know screamed like a Harpie from across the room.

"WHAT THE CRAP?!"

I am editing here. She used a different four-letter word from "crap." It also has four letters, and the root comes from the Middle Ages, more specifically the Middle Dutch word *fokken*, meaning "to thrust." Think about it.

As I opened my eyes, my roommate sat bolt upright in bed, cursing life, my cell alarm, and each individual member of the Spice Girls.

"AND TURN THAT THE CRAP OFF!"

I'm editing again.

I dashed out of bed to my cell on the desk where I slammed my hand down on the keypad to silence the alarm. Then I faced my new roommate for the first time.

I recognized her. She recognized me.

Chyna.

Chyna was Lori Williams.

"WHAT THE CRAP IS THE MATTER WITH YOU, YOU CRAPPING TWIT?"

Her thick hair hung in her face as she pointed at me. "You? *You?* You're my roommate?"

I was wide awake now. I went for maid-polite. "I'm sorry about the alarm. It won't happen again."

She didn't get out of bed, but she let her red satin sheet fall below her sumptuous breasts. I was in an old Chicago Bears T-shirt. She'd evidently slept in nothing.

"I'm Ronette Bradley," I added.

She dead-eyed me. "No you're not. You're the girl who I said better hope didn't go to Houseman. And you're the person who just wrecked my morning after I got in at five a.m. Get out."

"Excuse me?" I asked, not quite believing my ears.

"I said, get out. Get out of my room and let me sleep! Get your clothes, get your shoes, and get the crap out before I get out of bed and throw you the crap out!"

I had a choice to make. I could stand my ground and have a blowout with Chyna—I still wasn't sure how Chyna turned out to be Lori Williams, but I was sure there was a good answer. Or I could retreat and try to mend fences later.

In the hotel biz, they say never to get into an argument with a guest. Walk away if necessary.

"Okay. I'm out," I told her. "Gimme two minutes."

She stared at me, then dropped her head to her pillows and pulled the sheet over her face. I pulled on some jeans and a clean T-shirt, grabbed some kicks, my computer, my backpack, and my toothbrush, and was outta there in ninety seconds.

Fokken.

I got cereal and coffee in the McMaster dining room. Twenty minutes with my laptop and campus Wi-Fi gave me the 411 on Chyna. She was indeed Crystal's daughter. Her given name was Lori Williams. Her father had died in a plane crash when she was eleven. She'd picked the name Chyna for herself. She was a big party girl in New York. Everyone wanted her at their event or club. She'd done fashion shows, magazine shoots, and special appearances galore. Marta had been correct about the rehab. She'd been in and out of rehab like I was in and out of the shower.

She and Crystal didn't have a great relationship. In fact, Chyna had once gone to court to get herself declared an adult even though she was still a kid. She'd had famous boyfriends. Some were way older than she was.

This was my college roommate.

Later, I wrote about it in my notebook under "my" maple tree on the quad.

There's a time to apologize
To look a girl in the eyes
To forgo all the sighs, the lies, and the cutie pies
That we hide behind all the time.

There's a time to say okay
When a girl comes to apologize
To look you in your eyes;
Here's a word to the wise
Time flies, you get thunder thighs!
But words from the heart don't need to rhyme.

"Hey."

I looked up. Jayson stood over me. Like me, he was dressed casually and carried his backpack.

"Hey yourself," I said wearily.

"You don't sound so good."

"I'm not so good. You know that girl Chyna I dissed last night? She's my roommate."

"What? Get out of town!" He plopped down next to me.

"Yup. Lucky me. We got acquainted again this morning. Hate at second sight."

Jayson shook his head. "Man. I'd say talk to housing, but I bet she's doing it already. Maybe they'll move you. Or her. Or something. Want me to talk to her for you?"

I raised my eyebrows. "You? What could you possibly do?"

Jayson nodded slowly. "Good point. Just thought I'd offer."

I started to thank him, but a big crowd of kids making a whole lot of noise was gathering over by the flagpole. We decided to check it out. I put down my notebook and grabbed my backpack; then we hustled over. About a hundred kids formed a ring around the flagpole; they were shouting and clapping in rhythm.

"What's going on?" I asked Jayson.

Jayson grinned. "I'm not sure, but I think it's the Beta house."

A kid in front of us turned around. He was short with thick glasses. "It's the Betas for sure. This is gonna be good!"

I was still confused. "What's gonna be—"

Suddenly, a group of fifteen or twenty guys in matching purple T-shirts burst through the circle of students. They chanted rhythmically and formed two lines, dancing and chanting in perfect sync. Then, the two lines formed one big line, as the men put on an acrobatic performance of dance, shouting, chanting, and movement that got the whole crowd hollering.

"We the Beta house!" their leader announced. "Watch us steppin' and struttin'! All the rest of the houses, they be nuttin'!"

The performance continued. It could have been stupid, but it was actually cool watching these brothers. They'd obviously rehearsed for many hours, clapping and dancing just for the fun of it. It was worth writing about—

Omigod. My notebook.

I grabbed Jayson's arm. "Be right back!"

"Where you going?"

I was already gone, running across the quad to my tree, where I'd stupidly left my poetry notebook when I'd come with Jayson to watch the Betas do their thing.

I was hoping, praying it would still be there.

It wasn't.

My poetry notebook was gone.

Chapter Nine

$\mathcal{I}t's$ gone!" I wailed as Jayson ran up behind me.

"What's gone?"

"My notebook. I left it here when we went to watch the Betas. By mistake. All my poems are in it!"

Jayson saw how upset I was and took charge. "Okay, here's what we're going to do. I'm going to the left, and you're going to the right. We're gonna look everywhere and ask everyone if they saw it. Maybe someone picked it up. Is your name in it?"

I shook my head. I'd never put my name in it. There was no reason to. It was always with me. I'd never come close before to losing it.

"Well, you'll put your name in it now," Jayson joked lightly.

I wasn't in a laughing mood but was grateful for his help. "Let's get started. Stay in touch."

I decided to search the ground before I talked to anyone. I moved to my right, circling every tree. Nothing. There were shrubs behind the tree line. I looked under those, thinking maybe someone had tossed it away. Nothing. I wandered out onto the big lawn, hoping someone had moved it to where it could be seen more easily. Nothing.

Then I started talking. Freshmen and seniors. Maintenance staff guys in their black coveralls. Professors that happened to be passing by. I even saw two of the cheerleaders I'd met at the party.

"Hey, did you guys maybe see a notebook?" I asked.

One of the cheerleaders—I thought it was Shaneen, she had reddish hair pulled back in a ponytail and looked almost ordinary without her makeup—actually showed concern. "You lose one?"

"Under the tree over there." I pointed.

"Haven't seen anything," she told me. "But lost and found is in the basement of admin. You might want to check there. I lost my iPhone my first day and someone turned it in."

I thanked her profusely. "I'm Ronette. You're Shaneen, right?"

"That's right. Good memory."

"Thanks again, Shaneen."

"You're welcome. And save yourself some trips. Just call the college switchboard and ask to talk to them."

Huh. More helpful info. Maybe I'd misjudged her.

Jayson had no more luck than me. Even though it was getting close to time to go buy our books and finish registration, I did make one call to lost and found, like Shaneen had suggested. They said a sweatshirt, a set of keys, and a backpack had all been turned in today, but no notebook.

"Check the lost-and-found on the Houseman website. We log everything as it comes in," the guy told me.

Big points for efficiency. Zero for success.

"Why was I such an idiot?" I moaned to Jayson as we walked across campus to the field house where the book sale and registration would take place.

"Because you're human."

"I'm typing everything into my laptop the minute I finish it from now on," I vowed.

"How's your backup?" Jayson answered. "In case you lose your computer?"

I made a face. "Terrible."

He grinned. "So's mine. Let's get on that tonight."

"I'm checking the website every half hour," I promised.

It was a plan, but I still felt awful. There was a lot of good writing in that notebook. Some of it was pretty personal. I tried to remember if I'd mentioned Jayson by name in it. I didn't think so, but I could be wrong.

So. Registration and book buying. Picking college classes is mostly like in high school, where you make your choices and a computer sets it all up. But most places let you change your mind, and sometimes classes get added or have last-minute openings. Or if a person wants to study with a certain professor, it might be possible to talk that teacher into adding a spot. That's why Houseman has this Sunday session.

As for books, it's not at all like high school. In high school, the teacher hands out the books, which are owned by the school district. In college, students buy their own books. Some classes do have a textbook, but students have to buy that too. It can get expensive, so a lot of people look for used books, or computer files of textbooks, and that kind of thing. Today there'd be a book exchange and sale.

As we neared the field house, it seemed like every college kid in the country was heading over. We saw whole fraternities and sororities dressed alike. Some kids were in costume, making it a party. High school was never like this.

"Pretty cool, huh?" Jayson asked.

I'd recovered somewhat from the loss of my notebook. I figured it would get turned in to lost-and-found. What good would it do anyone else?

"I've never seen anything like it."

"Glad Houseman took you?"

I squeezed his arm tight. To be with my boyfriend, going to my first Houseman registration … well, nothing could be better.

Marta met us there. She was with the football kicker, Kevyn, and had dressed for combat: camouflage pants, a green Go Army T-shirt, and black boots. Kevyn wore black shorts and a black-and-white checked short-sleeve cotton shirt. He towered over her by a foot. They were a cute couple. And a couple they were. She had her arm looped through his. So much for her fears about never finding a boyfriend here.

We went down to the field house floor. Madness. Tables everywhere. Noisy as a basketball game. One side of the floor was for registration, the other side for books. I was already set up for freshman "baby" courses (so-called because they were the lowest level) in English, biology, French, and psychology. Also a course on the Civil War. Not a single class started before eleven in the morning. I could sleep in. Joy.

We stopped at a whiteboard of last-minute course changes, drops, and additions. I scanned it. A'ight. Then I saw something that was as good as losing my notebook was bad.

JUST ADDED: CREATIVE WRITING 401
(3 CR. MWF 5:00 PM)
PROF. SHAABAN LOWE
PRE-REGISTER W/PROF. LOWE HERE

Since when?

I pointed to the sign. "Look!"

"Look what?" Jayson asked.

"Shaaban Lowe is like, the best black poet ever. I didn't know he taught here. I've gotta take that!" I was thrilled.

Marta laughed. "Well, then I say get your fine Windy City ass moving!"

I needed no more prompting; I sped into the chaos, leaving my friends behind while I looked for Mr. Lowe. I knew about his work because my perceptive high school librarian suggested I read his books. Shaaban Lowe wrote about important stuff, but you didn't have to analyze his poems to death to understand them. You got them the first time, and then they got you.

Shaaban Lowe could be my teacher? This was crazy.

I found him at the far end of the field house floor, behind a desk with a sign on it about his class. He was tall, lanky, and had a huge Afro, glasses, and full beard. He wore an orange turtleneck even though the day was warm.

I wasn't the only Houseman student who wanted into his seminar. There was a line of fifteen or twenty kids that snaked forward very slowly. My feet hurt. But I was not going to miss the chance to have Shaaban Lowe critique my writing. It meant I'd be taking a ton of classes, but it would be worth it.

Finally, I stood before him. I admit it. I quaked.

He looked up at me. "Yes?"

I took a deep breath. "I'm Ronette Bradley and I would like to be in this class."

"Year?"

I almost said the date, but realized he wanted to know what year in school I was. "Freshman!"

He shook his head. "Sorry. Closed to freshmen. Next!"

Dammit. I hadn't realized that the seminar would be upperclassmen only. Still, I didn't move.

"Mr. Lowe, I don't know how to say this, but I *need* to be in your class. I know all your work. I've been reading you since I was in tenth grade. 'Harlem Rhapsody,' 'South-Central Rhapsody,' 'Rodney's Children,' 'In Memory of Claudette Colvin Before She Dies'—I've read 'em all."

He rubbed his bearded chin. "Nice Internet research."

"It isn't Internet research. I read every word!" I was talking from my heart now. "Mr. Lowe, this is impor-tant to me. It's like a sign that you're teaching here.

There's nothing that's more important to me than writing. Nothing!"

That got him. Kinda sorta.

"What did you say your name was again?" he asked.

"Bradley. Ronette Bradley. I'm from Chicago."

"Well, Ronette Bradley from Chicago, you are passionate about writing. That is a good thing. I am interested in passion. But this is an upper division seminar. I can't have you slowing down the room. How do I know you can even write?"

"I'll prove it to you."

The words were out of my mouth before I could think about them.

Mr. Lowe took a look at the restive line behind me. People were muttering and fidgeting. "You have something to show me?"

The answer would have been yes, if I hadn't lost my stupid notebook.

"No."

"Then I can't help you."

"How about if I write something for you right now?" I volunteered.

"Really?"

"Really," I told him. "Right now. I'll write a poem for you right now."

He beckoned to me; there was an open seat next to him. "Fine, Ronette Bradley from Chicago. Sit here and get to work. Let's see what you can do."

What could I do but move to the other side of the table, sit down, and take the paper and pencil he offered me? I stared at the whiteness of the paper. I was in it now.

Scary as the blank page was, I had no choice. I had to put words where my mouth was.

Chapter Ten

Fifteen minutes later, I cleared my throat. The line was gone, and Professor Lowe was messing around on his iPhone. "Professor Lowe?"

"Yes, Ronette Bradley?"

"I'm done." I slid the sheet of paper toward him.

What I'd written wasn't my best. Not by a long shot. I was too nervous. The setting for writing—this deafening, crowded field house—was too harsh. Foolishly, I was so nervous I didn't even think to open my laptop, where I had tons of old poems stored. He was going to read a first draft I'd dashed off in fifteen minutes. I didn't hold out much hope.

What I'd written was a variation on what I'd jotted in my notebook on the quad. I called it "Time to Apologize."

There's a time to apologize
To look a girl in the eyes
To skip the sighs, lies, and cutie pies
That we hide behind all the time.

There's a time to say okay
When it's time to apologize
To look a girl in her eyes
Here's a word to the wise
Time flies, you'll get thunder thighs!
But words from your heart
Don't need to rhyme.

Like I said, minor editing.

Mr. Lowe read it. Once. Twice. Three times.

"Who taught you to write, Ronette Bradley?" he asked me.

I shrugged a little. "Myself, I guess."

"You're a rookie," he declared.

My heart sank. But only for a moment.

"A rookie," he went on, "but there may be hope. Welcome to my seminar."

Was he kidding?

"I'm in?" I asked hesitantly.

"You're in. The dean will hand my head to me for this. But you're in."

He put his hand out. I shook it, big-time.

"Thank you, Professor Lowe. I mean it. I won't let you down."

He wrote out something on a form and signed it. "Take this to the registrar. See you tomorrow afternoon."

Omigod. I was in. I went to the registrar but ran into Marta before I got there. She was hauling a huge bag of books.

"Have you seen Jayson?" I asked. "I got into his class!"

"You got in!?" she echoed.

"I got in, I got in!"

She dropped the books and hugged me. "Haven't seen Jayson. Or Kevyn. Flaky guys. You got in!"

I went to the big registrar's desk and turned in the form for Shaaban Lowe's seminar. The registrar, an older man in a suit and tie with the first handlebar moustache I've ever seen on a black guy, was impressed.

"Shaaban Lowe taking a freshman into his seminar," he marveled. "How much did you have to bribe him?" Then he laughed. "Good for you, Ms. Bradley. Let's make this official."

He typed into his laptop. Then he frowned.

"Is there a problem?" I asked.

"Just that your tuition isn't paid. Deadline is Wednesday at five o'clock. Do what you need to do, Ms. Bradley."

Huh. Well, my mom had said that it would take a day or two to get the money. She'd have it taken care of by Monday, I figured. I'd be fine.

"It's fine, sir," I told the registrar.

"Good." He took something out of the printer and handed it to me. "There you go. Have you bought your books yet?"

I shook my head. He pointed to the left. "Over there. Welcome to Houseman."

I went to buy my books. Before I did, I found the quietest place in the field house—a nook directly behind a high stack of wrestling mats. I sat on the floor back there and called my mother.

Kalina picked up right away.

"Baby girl! Not forgettin' her mama back home. How are you, baby girl? How's my college girl?"

"I'm doin' great, Mama," I told her. "Everything's good. I just got into a writing class taught by Shaaban Lowe!"

"Who's he?"

My mother was never big on poetry. Remember how she believes that to write is to starve.

"He's—it's not important, Mama. I'm just happy."

"You taking any classes where you can actually earn a living?"

I did not want to get into that discussion.

"I'm a freshman," I reminded her. "There's a lot of required stuff."

"Oh." There was a pause. "How's Jayson? You have a roommate? How is she? You eatin' okay?"

"Good, good, and good," I lied. I didn't want to get into a Chyna discussion either. My mom was such a fan of Crystal's show. She'd give birth to my baby sister if she knew that Crystal's daughter was my roommate. Of course, for all I knew, Chyna might not be my roommate anymore. While I was at registration, she could have moved out.

"Well, that's good," Kalina allowed.

"Mama?"

"Yeah, baby girl?"

"You doing okay there all alone?"

Her voice was bright. "I'm fine, baby girl. Don't you worry none about me. Your mama can take care of herself."

"Okay." I hesitated and stretched my legs against one of the wrestling mats. "There is one more thing."

"What's that, sweetheart?"

"They just told me at registration that my tuition isn't in yet. Is everything okay with that?"

Kalina answered without hesitation. "Everything is fine. Perfect. It's just taking a day or two to get the money cleared. Bank's closed on the weekend, remember?"

"I remember."

She was right. She couldn't get the money on a Sunday. I breathed easier.

I heard muffled voices at the other end of the line. Then my mom came back to the phone.

"Baby girl? I'm working Sunday and the check-in rush is comin' on. Me and Alexis are busy. How about you call me later or tomorrow?"

"Okay, Mama."

"You be good, college girl."

"I will, Mama."

She clicked off.

I sat there on the floor with the cell in my hand for a moment. It had been weird talking to her. She felt very far away. It wasn't the seven hundred and fifty miles. It was more like I was talking to another lifetime.

I couldn't help thinking that I wasn't her baby girl anymore. I was now her college girl.

Jayson, Kevyn, Marta, and I had dinner in Hughes, the athletes' dorm. I have to say I've never seen such a fine crew of brothers in my life. The boys were workin' it. There were plenty of fly sisters too, attracted to the dark chocolate candy. The boys seemed to be eating up the attention.

After dinner, Jayson walked me back to McMaster.

"What'chu up to tonight?" he asked as we got to the front door.

"Sleep. Which is what you should be up to."

"Aww … I thought maybe we'd go into Adams-Morgan or even to Georgetown, see a movie or something. We'll be back by my curfew. Promise."

I shook my head. "No, no, and more no. Tomorrow's first day of class, and yours too. I'm not gonna do a repeat of Corman. I'm sleeping."

He laughed. "How can you be worried about sleeping? You don't have any classes till eleven o'clock!"

"True. But a girl needs her rest." I snaked my arms around his neck. "Movie on Friday night. I'll take you. How about that?"

He shook his head right back at me. "Not happening. Team travels to Hampton on Friday. First game of the season on Saturday. Remember?"

I winced. Yeah. Now I remembered. It was nice to have a football player boyfriend with guns of steel, but it was gonna mess with our social life.

"Don't worry," he told me. "We'll figure it out. How about I go back to my dorm now too? And sleep."

"I like that idea."

We kissed. We kissed again.

"Good luck tomorrow," I told him.

He flexed his biceps. "I don't need luck."

I went to my room. Chyna's gear still dominated the space. She hadn't moved out. I showered and got my stuff together for classes, then did a little reading in one of my new Civil War books. When I went to sleep at ten, Chyna hadn't come back.

The next morning, her bed was unwrinkled. Even though classes were starting, my roommate hadn't come home at all.

Chapter Eleven

By three o'clock on Monday afternoon, I was in a state of happy shock. College was nothing like high school. I was so excited that I called my mother, knowing it was two o'clock in Chicago and the check-in rush didn't start until three. She'd have time to talk. Plus, she had Skype and a camera on her smartphone, so if I used the webcam on my laptop, we could even see each other.

That's how I called her, setting up on battery power in the quad under my maple tree.

"Mama, I had to talk to you. I just had to! I'm so happy; this place is amazing! Thank you, thank you, thank you!"

My mother laughed at my joy. "Is that so, college girl? Tell me about it."

"I had English, baby biology, and psychology. All my professors are black. And two of them are women!"

My mother frowned. "You're taking a class about baby biology? What are they teaching you?"

I giggled like I was still in grade school. "No, no, Mama. It's just an intro course. Like, we freshmen are babies."

She relaxed visibly. "Oh. Good. 'Cause I don't need you learning about babies and getting ideas."

What is it about parents? Why is it they always get bent out of shape about all the wrong things?

"Don't worry, Mama," I told her. "To have a baby you have to do certain things, and me and Jayson aren't doing that, if you know what I mean."

"You don't have to lie, college girl. You stayed with him that night before he left for school. I know you two didn't tell bedtime stories and then roll over."

"We're not animals, Mama," I told her confidently. "Just because you do something once doesn't mean you have to do it again. Even if you like it."

"You just be careful," my mother cautioned.

She turned her head, as if to check a clock on the wall, and then came back to me. "How about your roommate? And the food? Are you eating? Making friends?"

This was my opening to tell her about Chyna. I did, in the most low-key way, leaving out how it was pretty much hate at first sight.

"Get down, Ronette!" My mother was dazzled. "I watch Crystal's show every day! She never talks about her daughter at college. She's your roommate? Are you sure? Maybe the girl's just makin' it up to shine you on."

Sometimes my mother had a light grip on reality. On the other hand, it was cool to see her so excited.

"It's her for sure."

"That's … that's great! Do you think that you'll meet her mother?"

"I don't know. It's possible, I guess."

"If you can, get me an autograph, okay? And one for Alexis too?"

"Okay, Mama." It was time to change the subject to something more pressing. "Mama?"

"Yes, college girl?"

"Everything still okay with my tuition? Because I have to pay by Wednesday."

My mother laughed maybe a bit too brightly. "It's fine! I'm working on it with the bank. It'll be paid on time. You just pay attention to school and make some friends."

"I am making friends," I assured her.

"And call your mama." She looked away again. "Okay, honey. I need to get back out to the desk. Alexis is out sick today, and we've got a new girl who doesn't know her left from her right. Bye, baby girl."

Aww. It felt good that she'd called me baby girl again. "Bye, Mama."

Looking back, I should have known right then that something wasn't right with my tuition. One thing about peeps, myself included: we're really good at not seeing things we don't want to see.

Instead of meeting in a classroom, Shaaban Lowe had chosen a side room in the college chapel as the location for his writing seminar. There were no desks, just couches, sofas, and a slew of pillows on the floor.

If I hadn't been so nervous, I might have appreciated the informal setting. But the curious—and, on a couple of faces, hostile—stares from the other kids made me sweat. I was glad that I'd worn black jeans and a black T-shirt. Black doesn't show perspiration.

It was obvious that the kids knew each other. No one knew me. But it seemed like the word was out that there was a lowly freshman in their midst. I found myself on a chair, unable to get comfortable, all alone in one corner.

Professor Lowe came in right at the top of the hour. He wore dark slacks and an open-collar white shirt. He looked younger than at registration. I knew from my reading that he was in his late forties. Everyone shut up the second he entered the room.

"Good afternoon, I'm Shaaban, and now that you're my students, don't call me Mr. Lowe or even Professor Lowe. The only people who call me Mr. Lowe are my dentist and the DMV, and I don't like going to either place. As for 'Professor Lowe,' there is no reason to impress or flatter me. You are already here. This is a creative writing seminar, and you are fortunate to be in it."

A hand went up immediately. Not mine. A girl with long dreadlocks, a long blue dress, and about fifty jangly necklaces. "Shaaban?"

Shaaban waved her off. "Whoever you are, I don't take questions when I'm talking. In fact, I ask them. Right now, I want you to call out the names of writers you love."

The names came fast and furious, though as a freshman I kept my mouth shut. Zora Neale Hurston. Langston Hughes. John Edgar Wideman. James Baldwin. Maya Angelou. Toni Morrison.

As my classmates shouted names, I watched Shaaban get more and more vexed. He stomped around the room, all the while asking for even more names. I couldn't understand why he seemed so frustrated. These were all great black writers.

Finally, he could take no more.

"Stop! Stop, stop, stop!" he thundered as he strode into the center of the lounge. "What is wrong with you people?"

The room fell silent. I was still baffled. What was the problem?

Shaaban proceeded to tell us what the problem was.

"I will have no bigots or racists in my classroom! There are twenty-five of you. I heard many names. Not a single white writer. Not a Latino. Not a South American. Not a Russian. You are naming writers you love and no one says Joyce? Molière? Chekhov? David Foster Wallace? Anne Lamott? Carson McCullers? Isaac Bashevis Singer? No! I will not have it! I will not have a classroom of bigots!"

He moved to an empty seat and sat.

The rest of the class was spent in silence. I'm serious. Not a sound. None of us dared to speak or leave, and Shaaban had nothing else to say. I got the sense that he was testing us.

The silence gave me a chance to study my classmates. It was half guys and half girls. There seemed to be two distinct groups of kids. One was clustered around a good-looking tall guy with glasses and thick eyebrows, the other kept looking toward the girl with the dreads. It was almost like there were two teams of students. Strange.

Finally, at the end of our "hour" (hour-long college classes meet for fifty minutes), Shaaban spoke again.

"Between now and next class, I want you to write about what happened in here today," he said conversationally. It was like his anger was forgotten. "Dig deep. If you're writing a poem, I want no more than a hundred words. If a scene, no more than three hundred words. I hate blather, and college students seem to think their every word is gold. Nonsense. E-mail your work to me by five tomorrow in a Word file; I'll compile and distribute. Read everyone's and come prepared to discuss. That's it. We're done."

He got up and walked out. The moment he was gone, the kids broke into heated debate over the weird first class we'd just had.

No one looked at me. Neither "coach" seemed to want me on their team.

Fine. I had studying to do and a poem to write.

When I left the lounge, the other kids were still arguing.

On the way out, I got a call from a local number. My caller ID said it was the Houseman bursar's office.

"This is Ronette," I answered.

It was a robo-call. "This is a friendly reminder from the Houseman Office of the Bursar to any and all students who have not settled their accounts with our department. All tuition must be paid in full by five p.m. on Wednesday. No exceptions. Thank you."

I made a face. My tuition obviously hadn't been paid. My mother had to come through. She just had to.

Chapter Twelve

I did something unusual after dinner my first night of classes.

I studied.

Back in Chicago, I loved to read but hated to study. Reading was easy. I would go to the public library and scan the shelves, looking for something with an interesting title or cover. I didn't care what it was about. Astronomy. North Africa. Fashion. Politics. Economics. Sometimes I would even take a volume of the old print encyclopedias, open it at random, and read that. No muss, no fuss, no test.

I know. I'm weird.

It is a fact I did less well with stuff that was assigned to read. I mostly didn't read it. By the time I got to high school, teachers stopped caring that I didn't read my assignments. There were plenty of kids at Corman who were flunking. I was just another girl who didn't live up to my potential.

I knew that I had to change if I was going to succeed in college.

I would like to report that everything I got assigned to read was so interesting that it was easy for me to change my ways, but that was not the case. In baby English, we were starting with short stories by a dead white guy, Ernest Hemingway. In bio, I had a textbook. Ditto psychology.

Boring. How was I going to learn this material?

It turned out that my new bestie, Marta, was a studying genius.

We'd settled in at a basement table in the library. I was starting in on the Hemingway my usual way. Fast. No notes. Marta interrupted me.

"What are you doing?" she asked crossly.

"Reading Hemingway."

She shook her head. "That won't help you. You can't read it. You have to study it. Look." She pointed to her own work. She was in baby political science and had a book about the history of Congress. "You need to take notes. Then you use those notes when you study instead of messing with the book. You need to make outlines as you go."

"That'll take forever!" I protested.

"That's why we have so much free time. To study. Ronette, you need to study three hours for every hour of class. That's what my dad told me, and he's right."

"Did he go to college?" I asked.

Marta nodded. "Of course. Florida State. So he could go into the military as an officer."

I winced. "My mom barely finished high school."

"Got it. So she didn't have the proper study tools to teach you. We can fix that. I'll work with you, but I can't do it *for* you. You gotta be willing to do the work. Dealy?"

I nodded gratefully. "Dealy."

For the first time in my life, I had a study buddy.

Marta showed me her method. She taught me how to set up an outline and use the same style for all of them. We studied until almost ten. Studied. It was grueling. My right hand actually got stiff from taking notes. But when I was done with the first Hemingway short story and my psych homework, I had two good outlines done Marta's old-fashioned way, with Roman numerals and capital letters and numbers and small letters.

I felt proud. I felt like a real college student. Then Marta asked a surprising question.

"I'm going to the Gamma house for a meet-and-greet. Wanna come with?"

"I'd never guess you were a sorority type," I joked as we climbed the stone steps to the Gamma sorority house. Houseman had both a "fraternity row" and a "sorority row" near the library. The Gamma house was the central house on sorority row. Greek members lived and ate in their houses, while everyone else lived in regular dorms like McMaster.

"I'm not sure I am," Marta confessed. "But this girl in my poli-sci class—Jacey—said her older sister, Nola, is prez of the Gammas. She invited me. She said all this great stuff, like they have the best dining room and all the old school tests on file so members can use them. Papers that sisters have written too. So I thought, why not?"

"Because it's segregation," I told her. "Voluntary segregation."

"If it's voluntary, it's not segregation. Besides, I think boys can be a distraction," she said.

I thought of Jayson. "Yeah."

I went inside with Marta, though. I figured it was good to try new things. That was one of the reasons I was at Houseman. If I wanted the same old, same old, I could just scrub barf off hotel room floors.

To my surprise, I had a good time. The Gamma girls all wore black-and-white striped shirts so we freshmen could pick them out of the big crowd. They were great hosts, making sure everyone was happy, passing food and drinks, taking people on tours, and the like.

Marta and I were just starting to look around when someone called to her.

"Marta! Hey!"

We stopped and turned around. A massively thick girl with a winning smile was waving at us. She had kind eyes and wore a low-cut black dress that emphasized her impressive chest.

"Hey, Jacey!" Marta waved back. "Come here, I want you to meet my friend Ronette from Chicago. She's the one I told you about."

Marta had been talking about me as a friend? Nice.

Jacey came over, started to shake my hand, and then hugged me. "If you're Marta's girl, forget that handshake bull. You get hugged. Your friend is the bomb, by the way."

"I know it," I told her.

"What do you think of Houseman?" she asked me. "Different from Chicago I bet. What are you taking? How's your roommate? How'd you talk your way into Shaaban Lowe's class? I heard he wasn't going to take any freshmen. And how do I get a boyfriend as fine as yours?"

I liked this girl already. I started to answer the question about Chicago, but then the lights flickered.

"Oops, we'll catch up another time. Time for the big

show!" Jacey announced. "Follow me."

She led us to a spacious rear meeting room. The walls were covered with homecoming banners from years past, plus signs from rush week and various other Greek activities. The room was jammed with excited freshmen girls.

Oh no. Chyna.

I spotted her across the way, holding court in the center of a cluster of worshipful girls. She didn't see me. Thank God.

Jacey was right. The Gammas put on a show.

First her sister, Nola, came out to welcome everyone. She was as thin as Jacey was thick, but with the same winning smile and friendly manner. She wore the Gamma uni for the night—a black-and-white striped shirt with black trousers—as she took her place on a low stage.

"We're just glad you're here," she told us. "Rush doesn't start till January, but that don't mean you can't get to know us. Being a Gamma isn't for everyone. Each of our girls is outstanding in her own way. If you do become a Gamma, you're a Gamma for life. Word is, there's a Gamma chapter in heaven too!"

Everyone laughed. Jacey beamed. Marta seemed entranced. I had to admit I was at least a little interested.

"So, let's get this party started!"

Without any warning, all the Gamma girls moved to the stage and lined up. The steppin' and struttin' began. All I can say is that it put the Beta boys I saw on the quad to shame. These proud black women were together, having fun, raising the roof. We girls who were watching picked up the rhythms and rhymes, dancing and prancing ourselves. I was right in the middle of the action, having a good old time.

When the steppin' and struttin' finished, Nola took the stage again.

"We Gammas know how to get down!"

Everyone cheered.

"To be a Gamma, you got to be able to bring it. So I ask you, wannabe-Gammas. Anyone ready to bring it? Right here? Right now?"

Silence.

Then Chyna's hand went up. "I'll bring it! If you can set up my beats!"

"Who are you?" Nola asked.

I don't know if Nola was ignorant about Chyna or faking it for the rest of us.

Chyna pushed her way through the crowd. Actually, it parted like the Red Sea for Moses. She wore a designer gray dress with a thick black leather belt and lace-up black boots. She handed an iPhone to Nola. "You'll know me soon enough. Dock this up, and we can get this party started!"

"That's my roommate," I confided to Jacey.

"Chyna? You're kidding! Lucky you."

"If she's gonna do hip-hop, cover your ears," I suggested sourly, remembering Chyna's last lame-ass performance.

The Gammas had an ace sound system for parties in the meeting room. In no time, the speakers pounded out a heavy bass dub. Then Chyna started to rap:

> *You feelin' so sad*
> *'Cause you think you been had*
> *It makes you feel mad*
> *Opp'site of bein' glad*
> *You look in the mirror*
> *Don't like what'chu see*
> *'Cause the reason that you mad*
> *Starin' right where you be!*

Jacey was dancing and bopping.

Marta poked me in the ribs. "She's good!"

Me? I was stunned. Seething. Furious. I knew those words. They were mine!

It can change in a instant
It change on a dime
Your phone be ringing
"Honey here's a good time
To get your ass outta town to a place
You wanna be
Not New York, not LA, but just
The Dee Cee!"

As the crowd went nuts and Chyna soaked in the love, I grabbed Marta's sleeve. "I gotta get out of here."

"Where you going?" she asked. "Enjoy the show!"

"I'll call you. I gotta go!"

I pushed my way out through the crowd, so angry I could barely see straight. Chyna had stolen my poem. No way was she gonna get away with it.

Chapter Thirteen

$\mathcal{I}$ ran all the way across campus to McMaster and took the stairs three at a time to my dorm room. Once inside, I didn't hesitate. I had one shot at proving that Chyna ripped me off, which was to find my notebook before she knew I was looking for it.

The more I thought about it, the more likely it seemed that it would be in the room. No way she'd carry it with her. Too easy to get busted. Freshmen weren't allowed to have cars, so she couldn't keep it in her trunk. Where else could it possibly be but here? Plus, from her point of view, she had no idea it was mine. I was sure she was planning to take more of my work and pass it off as her own.

I dug through her gear and her life. Carefully at first, so that she wouldn't know I'd been looking. I pawed through her drawers and searched her closet. Moved her shoes in case the notebook was underneath. Checked behind her vanity. On her shelves. Behind her bed.

I saw all kinds of stuff. Pills. 420. Money. But not what I was looking for.

Fokken.

I got more frantic, knowing that my time was limited. Where could the damn thing be?

I yanked up the pricey rug. Stuck my hands between her mattress and her box spring. Checked for bulges behind the hip-hop wall posters and under her sub-woofer.

Nothing. Where the hell was it?

I had just pulled back her bedspread when the door opened.

Chyna.

Busted.

Guiltily, I flung back the covers, but she had caught me red-handed.

"What the crap are you doing?" she thundered. "Get the crap out of my stuff!"

"You have something that belongs to me. I'm looking for it," I huffed back.

She flung her red Birkin bag on the bed and jammed her hands to her hips. "Oh, really? That's rich. Then why don't you tell me what it is!"

Was she really going to play dumb? Fine. Let her.

"I was just at the Gamma house. You know that rap you did? It wasn't yours. You didn't write it. You stole it."

Chyna barked a laugh. "Ha! Really. Stole it from who?"

"From me! I wrote it. It was in my poetry notebook. I don't know how you got my notebook, but you got it. You stole my poem. Everyone thought you were so ace. But you didn't write it!"

Chyna sat down on her bed and grinned like this was the funniest thing in the world.

"You think I took your notebook. And that I took your rap."

"That's right." I held my ground.

"Prove it."

I looked down at the floor. I was hoping she wouldn't ask me that.

"I can't prove it. I wish I could. I left my notebook on the quad yesterday. By mistake. I reported it to lost-and-found, but it never got turned in. Now I know why."

Chyna started to unlace her boots. It took a long time. I waited for her to say something else. That took a long time too. "Ronette, I'm going to say it again. Prove it."

"All right. Listen. Here it is."

I closed my eyes and tried to see my poem in my mind's eye. I'd never been that good at memorizing. This would have been a good time for me to improve. I'd have to do the best I could.

> *You feelin' so sad*
> *'Cause you think you been had*
> *It makes you feel mad*
> *Opp'site of bein' glad*
> *You look in the mirror*
> *Don't like what'chu see*
> *'Cause the reason that you mad*
> *Starin' right where you be!*

That was as much as I could pull up. I opened my eyes, hoping for a Hamlet moment—that by hearing me recite my poem, Chyna might be overcome with remorse the same way that King Claudius felt guilty after he saw the play that Hamlet rewrote.

Fat chance. Instead, she clapped.

"Bravo, bravo. You have superior listening skills. Or maybe my words were just so powerful." Then she got in my face. "I could have you arrested, you heifer. Keep your damn hands out of my stuff."

"With what you've hidden in this room, I could have you arrested too," I fired back.

"Wouldn't be the first time, won't be the last," she said

nonchalantly. "But I'm in a good mood tonight, so I'm gonna let you off the hook. From what I hear, you're not gonna be around this place much longer anyway."

"What do you mean?"

"I mean, Ronette Bradley from Chicago, if you don't pay your tuition by the end of Wednesday, they're kicking you out of school. Which means I'm gonna get me a new roommate. It can't happen too soon." She flounced back to her bed and pulled her dress over her head. Her underwear was all French lace.

How did she know that I hadn't paid tuition? Then I realized that was such a stupid question. When you're Chyna, I figured you just knew things.

There was nothing more to say. She'd stolen my poem and had my notebook, but I couldn't prove it. Without proof, there was nothing more I could do. And she was right—if my tuition wasn't paid by Wednesday, the whole thing would be moot anyway.

I didn't want to look at her perfect face and perfect chest in her perfect French lace bra one more second.

"I'm outta here," I told her.

"Good for you, don't come back," were her parting words.

I banged the door shut behind me.

Where to go?

I headed for the Grind, the coffee joint in the library's annex. Jayson didn't have to be at bed check for another forty-five minutes, so I sent him a frantic text.

"Pls mt me. Grind now!"

He texted back a quick okay and was at a round table for two when I got there. He wore baggy olive shorts, flip-flops, and a Houseman football T-shirt. He'd already ordered a couple of decafs. The place was crowded with students on study break.

"Damn, you look like hell," he told me, then embraced me. "Talk."

I did. I told him everything, starting with my tuition problems, and then the whole story about Chyna, my poem, and our showdown.

When I was done, he took my hand. "That's just wack."

"I know she has it."

He held up a hand. "You can't be sure. I mean, you can be sure it's your poem, but if I were her, I'd have copied what I wanted and then burnt that notebook. Or tossed it."

I hadn't thought of that. "Yeah. I guess you're right."

"Anyway, it's a lost cause now. You need to think about the tuition thing."

"I know!"

He sipped his decaf. "I bet your mom's gonna come through. Just relax."

"I hope so."

My stomach was in too many knots to want decaf. Plus, there was something unsaid here. His dad had plenty of money. They were as rich as Jay-Z. He could loan it to me. All it would take was a phone call. I wouldn't want a gift. Just a loan. I'd pay it back when I started working again.

I didn't ask Jayson, though. It's not the kind of thing you ask your boyfriend for. And Jayson didn't volunteer. So we just sat there, holding hands.

For the moment, that was the best I could do.

Chapter Fourteen

Like a dead white guy once wrote, it was the best of times and the worst of times.

The big issue for the next two days was tuition. It had to be paid or my ass was outta there. No way around it. No way to bend the rules. I wasn't mad at the school about it. I guessed how much it had to cost to run a place like that. Plus, tuition was fair compared to other colleges.

On Tuesday, after I wrote and uploaded my poem for Shaaban Lowe's seminar, I called my mom.

"Don't worry, college girl," she told me. "I said I'd have it covered, and I'm gonna have it covered. If not today, tomorrow. You do your regular thing and let your mama do her thing."

When a mother tells you not to worry, it's a sign to do the opposite. But I knew worrying would not help my cause. It's not like I could come up with almost thirteen grand myself. My fate was in my mother's hands.

I tried to do "my regular thing." On Wednesday, I went to my classes and downloaded and read all the stuff my writing seminar classmates had turned in by e-mail. Shaaban had assembled it all into one big PDF.

I gulped when I read through the printout I made at the campus computer center. Shaaban had asked that we write about what had happened in his seminar on Monday when we'd sat for so long in silence. I had completely forgotten his instructions and wrote about something else. Everyone else had done what he'd asked. He'd placed my poem last in the handout. Probably he would tear me a new one.

"I wonder if he'll kick me out for messing up," I said to Marta. We were eating lunch on the quad. Every day the food service sent out trucks with different kinds of ethnic food. We could get lunch by scanning our food service cards. These trucks were crazy popular; lunch on the quad is as much a Houseman tradition as steppin' and struttin'. Marta and I had picked up chicken burritos, refried beans, and iced tea. Latino soul food.

"Doubt it. He'll just think you're a stupid freshman."

I made a face. "Great. Very helpful. Everyone will laugh at my ass." I took a swallow of iced tea. My mouth had gone dry with nerves.

"Let's say no one laughs at you. Let's say he even loves what you did. You still can't tell if your poem is any good. That's why I like elections," Marta declared.

A breeze came up; she buttoned the top button of the paisley shirt she wore, which matched her bright green leggings. Somehow, Marta made this retro look work. I had on black jeans and a plain white T-shirt. A lot of Houseman kids dressed up to go to class, but I liked to be comfortable. Not that it mattered. This could be my last day of Houseman classes ever if my mom didn't come through for me. I'd decided not to call and bug her. What would be the point? All I could do was "my regular thing" and hope.

"We're not talking about elections," I told Marta. "That's your department. You're the poli-sci major."

"At least in elections," she shot back, "you know who wins. It's not a matter of opinion. I mean, before Election Day, everyone is flapping their gums and whatnot, but finally you count the votes and the person with the most votes wins. It's not a matter of opinion. Unlike writing. Just because Shaaban Lowe likes a poem doesn't make it good. And just because he hates it doesn't make it bad."

"Come on," I chided her. "There's good music and bad. Good art and bad. Good writing and bad. Good food and bad. Take this burrito. It's damn good."

I took a huge bite; beans and chicken spilled out.

"That *looks* like a good burrito," Marta agreed. "But how can I know? Under your theory, because it tastes good to you means it *is* good to me."

I laughed. "Good point. But in my world, what Shaaban Lowe thinks is good *is* good. So we'll have to agree to disagree."

Marta rolled her eyes, then said, "Um, I hate to be the voice of reality here, but what are you going to do if your tuition doesn't get paid?"

I swallowed hard, even though my mouth had no food in it. "I don't know."

"I wouldn't know either. Have you called the bursar? Or your mom?"

I wiped my lips with a paper napkin. "No. It won't make a difference. Whatever's going to happen is going to happen."

By five o'clock, the time of Shaaban's seminar, I was actually feeling better. I hadn't heard from the bursar. I figured that had to mean my tuition was paid. Once again, I found myself sitting alone in the chapel lounge while the other kids gathered around the same two seniors as last time—the sister with the dreads and the fine brother with the eyebrows. This time, the guy gave me a little wave. I waved back shyly. The girl paid me no mind.

Shaaban entered the lounge. He had on jeans and a blue work shirt with his sleeves rolled up; he carried a dark blue briefcase. Talk stopped. He sat on a folding chair, opened his briefcase, and took out a sheaf of papers that had to be our writing.

"Let's start," he declared. "Here's how it works. I call on you. You read your piece. Your classmates react. I react. You go home, you rewrite, you submit for next class along with a new piece. It means nothing if I don't call on you. You'll get your chance another time. Rewrite anyway. Ronette Bradley?"

Omigod.

He was starting with me. Was he going to make an example of me of how not to write? Of how not to follow directions in college? Why hadn't I listened? Sure, I could blame it on the tuition thing, or the Chyna thing, but the bottom line was the same. I'd messed up.

I raised my hand. It shook.

Shaaban pointed at me. "Stand. Read."

I wanted to say no, that he should start with a senior. Or even a junior. Instead, I said nothing; I just sat there with the papers shaking in my hand.

"Ronette? You have two choices. Read or withdraw from my class," he told me. "I suggest the former."

There were titters and whispers. I stood. The papers in my hand still flapped like the wings of a baby sparrow.

"Disgrace"

For the longest time, since Appomattox
They'd point to us and say, "Know your place!"
Don't be too loud, don't be too proud
Don't crowd, just stand there and be cowed
While your world goes up in a mushroom cloud.

Now times have changed, it's safe if you're queer
There's a black man in the White House
No need to feel fear
No excuse to be two face, in a bad place
Act real to your race; no one so much a reverse ace
As a rich girl disgrace.
As a rich girl disgrace.

My poem went on for another verse, then swung back around to the last two lines again.

"Act real to your race; no one so much a reverse ace as a rich girl disgrace. As a rich girl disgrace."

I finished. Silence.

"Reactions?" Shaaban asked. "One word reactions. Call them out!"

I could barely look at their faces. I've got a good vocab, but some of these words I didn't even know. The ones I did know made me feel awful.

"Puerile!"

"Pedantic!"

"Derivative!"

"Expected!"

Brutal comments made worse since I didn't even write on the correct topic.

Someone said, "Moving!" but it barely registered.

Finally, the comments ended. Shaaban stepped forward.

"You have proved yourselves to be poor critics," he told the class. "*I* liked it a lot. It has a beat, it has heart, the rhymes are good, and I really liked the 'mushroom cloud' thing." He turned to me. "Do more of that, Ronette. And learn to follow directions."

Omigod.

He liked it. Shaaban Lowe liked my poem!

I beamed. Now, I looked at my classmates. Many of them scowled, except for the tall guy. He smiled at me. I smiled back. Shaaban made a few suggestions for my rewrite—he wanted me to be more specific about time and place and make more historical references—then told me to sit down.

I did, but I was flying for the next forty-five minutes. It barely registered who else read or what their stuff was about. The only poem I paid any attention to was by the tall guy with the thick eyebrows. His name was Cornell. He wrote about what it had been like to listen to the silence. I thought it was deep.

Then class was over.

I was on my way out when Cornell called to me. "Ronette!"

I turned. He was smiling at me again.

"Hi, I'm Cornell. I loved what you wrote."

"You didn't call it 'puerile'?" I asked.

He shook his head. "Moving, I think. Good job."

I grinned. "Thanks. I liked yours too. You're a really good writer."

He nodded. "Thank you. Anyway, I'm the editor of *The House*, the school literary journal. I'd love for you to join."

Oh. My. God.

"I'd like that!" I didn't try to hide my enthusiasm.

"And I'd like to have coffee with you. That is, if you don't have a boyfriend," he added almost shyly.

"I have a boyfriend," I confessed, almost regretfully. "He goes to school here too. He's from Chicago, like me."

"Well, I hope he appreciates his talented girlfriend. I'll talk to you next time about the magazine. Give you a few copies. Go ahead and Google it. It's pretty cool. Listen, lemme give you my digits. If you join the magazine, you'll need 'em."

We swapped numbers. Then we stood awkwardly.

"Okay. Good job, Ronette," he said again. "See you."

He loped away.

Well then. I had been asked out by a senior. That I couldn't or wouldn't go was beside the point. It had happened. I floated out of the chapel. I floated down the stairs. I would have floated to the quad and back to my room if my cell hadn't sounded.

It was the bursar. And this time it was *not* a robo-call.

"Ronette, can you come in immediately? There's a problem."

I went straight to the admin building, the good times of writing class forgotten. I was about to get kicked out of school. I broke down and called my mother on the way. No answer.

I had to wait in line at the bursar. It was sobering. Other kids obviously had tuition problems too. I stood numbly. I had no idea what I was going to do after I got the news. Cry probably. Then what? How could I even go home to Chicago when I didn't have money for a plane ticket? Bus? How soon would I need to be out of the dorm?

It was horrible.

Finally I reached the front. The older woman was no-nonsense. She asked me my name.

"Ronette Bradley."

Her eyes grew wide.

"You're Ronette Bradley?" She turned to the maze of cubicles and desks behind her where a bunch of other people were working. "Hey! This is the girl! This is Ronette!"

All the secretaries and helpers stopped work to stare at me. Some even came out of their cubicles to check me out. I had no idea why.

"You, um, called me," I stammered.

"I did," the woman reported. "I called because there was a problem with your tuition. Past tense. Was." She reached into a file folder. "You have friends in high places, Ronette Bradley. This just got messengered over."

She handed me a check payable to Houseman University for twelve thousand five hundred dollars.

The check was drawn on Crystal Enterprises, New York, New York. The signature at the bottom was neat, clear, and unmistakable. Crystal Williams. The famed talk show host. The mother of my roommate.

Crystal had just paid my tuition.

Chapter Fifteen

The next thing I thought was that this was some kind of cruel joke.

Chyna. Of course. Of course she'd do something like this. I figured she had a bunch of her mother's checks, maybe on an old account. When the bursar went to deposit it, the check would bounce higher than the Washington Monument. Or maybe Chyna had mocked up a check on her computer, printed it, and sent it over here to mess me up.

"Are you sure it's real?" I asked the bursar.

She nodded. "Real as you and me. We called the bank. It's good. Your tuition is paid." She peered at me. "Can I ask you something?" She plunged on without waiting for my permission. "How do you know Crystal? Is she a family friend or something?"

"It's a long story."

Yeah. That was for damn-ass sure. One that I didn't completely understand. Yet, anyway.

"Well, you're a lucky girl," the bursar told me. She glanced beyond me to the next kid in line—a girl with worry lines between her eyes that looked like double upside down hockey sticks. She was probably in tuition trouble. Somehow, I didn't think Crystal had messengered over a check for her too.

The bursar smiled. "I'm sure it is. Well, that's all for you, Ronette. Have a good year."

I tightened my backpack on my shoulder and hustled out of the building. There were two things I needed to do.

First, talk to my mother.

Second, talk to my not-so-beloved roommate.

It turned out that my mom still couldn't or wouldn't answer her cell. Chyna, though, was in the room when I burst in. She was on her bed with her eyes closed, bopping to something playing through earbuds. As usual, she was in her underwear. Gray silk, this time.

The girl did have some fantastic slam-dunks.

"Chyna!"

Nothing.

I did the logical thing. I yanked the earbuds out of her

ears. Her eyes snapped open. "Hey! What the crap are you doing?"

"We need to talk."

"Go to hell." She pushed her earbuds back in.

I pulled them out again. "I mean it. We need to talk!"

"You've been kicked out? Great, let's talk." She sat up. One of the earbuds dropped into her impressive cleavage. "What do you want?"

"Why did your mother just pay my tuition?"

Finally, I'd said something that made her take notice. She gave me a really weird look. "Can you repeat that?"

I put my hands on my hips. "I just came from the bursar's office. There was a check from your mother for my tuition. Twelve thousand five hundred dollars, which is what I owe. I want to know what the hell is going on."

She kept looking at me strangely. Then she roared with laughter so loud that the Obama girls had to hear it over in the White House. "Omigod! Ronette! You got me! You totally got me! I believed you! No one ever gets me and you got me! You go, girl!"

She laughed more. When I didn't join in, though, she quieted. Meanwhile, I was forming a theory.

"You're serious," she said.

I gave one big nod. "Do you think I could make this up? Your. Mother. Paid. My. Tuition. And I think I know why."

"Huh." Chyna shrugged. "If she did, I have no clue. Maybe she's having a bipolar episode. I wouldn't put it past her. She's great at putting on a show."

"That's not it. I think you told her to do it," I accused.

"Are you nuts!?" Chyna went to her closet and found yet another silk robe. This one was purple. "Why would I do that?"

"Because you feel guilty you stole my poem, that's why!" I followed her, blocking her near the closet with my body.

"You're back on that?"

"You did it and you know it!"

"Okay. Let's say I did it," Chyna practically spat. "If I did it, why the crap would I want you around, Ronette? Think! The last thing I'd do would be to get her to pay your tuition! And if I wanted to make nice—which I don't!— I'd pay it myself!" She pushed past me and went back to her bed.

I had to admit she had a point. A couple of points, actually. But who knew how this girl's mind worked? I sure didn't.

"I don't understand why, but I still think you told her," I declared.

Chyna sighed the mother of all sighs. "Jeez, Ronette. You do not give up, do you? I didn't want to do this, but …"

She didn't finish the sentence. Instead, she got her iPhone and flipped to one of her contacts. All I could do was listen in as she talked to whoever answered.

It was her mother.

"Mom? It's me," Chyna said, glaring at me the whole time. "Look, I'm with my roommate and she says you just paid her Houseman tuition … Uh-huh … Uh-huh … Uh-huh … I see. … Okay. Hold on."

She thrust her cell at me. "She wants to talk to you."

I rode up alone in the elevator at the Four Seasons Hotel. I was headed to the penthouse where Crystal was waiting for me.

The past hour had me in a daze. I'd had a short conversation with the famed talk show host. She confirmed that she had paid my tuition and said she wanted to see me. She was in Washington to interview the First Lady for her show and staying at the Four Seasons. Could she send a car to get me?

Chyna smirked at me the whole time. She had nothing more to say. In fact, she put her earbuds back in and closed her eyes again. I didn't yank them out.

I'd thought about changing before going downstairs to meet the car service, but then decided not to. I was who I was; I wasn't about to dress up. I stepped out when the elevator doors opened. The floor had a guard desk. The young Asian woman wore a regular hotel uniform, but I had no doubt she was packing under that jacket.

"May I help you?" she asked.

"Crystal's room, please."

"Your name?" she queried.

"Ronette Bradley."

She checked a list and saw my name.

"Suite four, Miss Bradley," she instructed, then pointed. "Down that corridor."

My heart pounded as I made my way to Crystal's suite. There was a white doorbell next to the carved, ornate door. I pressed it and heard gentle chimes from within.

The door opened.

There she was, dressed in a black pants suit with her hair tied back neatly in a bun.

No, not Crystal.

My mother.

Chapter Sixteen

My mother?

My eyes had to be messing with me. I squinted and refocused as my breath caught in my throat. I felt a shock of electricity course through me from brain stem to toes and back again. This was impossible. My mother was not in the Dee Cee. She could not be in the Dee Cee.

Wrong. She was right in front of me. Her face went from loving to sheepish to concerned to hesitant.

It stayed on hesitant.

"What are you doing here?" I yelped.

"I … I …"

My mother couldn't meet my eyes. In fact, she swung around toward Crystal, who was a foot or two behind her. The big star was taller than I imagined—probably close to five foot nine. She wore a stunning linen shirt and comfortable brown trousers. Her face—one of the most well-known in the world—was unlined. Maybe it was makeup, maybe it was Botox, or maybe she just had great genes.

"Come in, Ronette," Crystal beckoned in that famous voice of hers. "This has to be strange for you. There's tea and cookies in the living room. I'll explain everything."

Strange was the understatement of the year.

Three minutes later I was in the living room of her stunning suite. It was more like an apartment than a hotel room. From the living room I could see a full kitchen, and a hallway that led to probably a couple bedrooms— larger than my Chicago apartment by a lot. The décor was modern, with floor to ceiling windows that looked out on the city. In the distance I could see the Capitol. There was even a white-uniformed attendant who poured the tea and placed three thin cookies on my plate.

"I suppose you want to know everything." Crystal's voice was disarming.

"You could say that." I turned to my mother. "Mama, what are you doing here?"

"Kalina, why don't you tell her?" Crystal prompted, the same way she'd get a guest to speak up on her show. "I'll fill in the gaps."

My mother nodded. I could see this was hard for her. I wanted to fire off more questions, but I waited for my mom to speak.

"Ronette," she said. Her eyes were moist. "I love you so much, baby girl. When you got into Houseman, I was so happy for you. So proud. There was no way that I wasn't going to make sure you could go. Even if I didn't have the money to send you."

Didn't have the money.

What was she saying?

"I thought there was a rainy day fund," I responded carefully.

She shook her head. "No fund. You know we don't have a buried bone. It's always been paycheck to paycheck."

I did know that. But when she'd said "rainy day money," I'd hoped …

"I figured—I prayed—that I could get the money somehow. I didn't want you to worry. I'd ask friends, I'd borrow it, I'd talk to the hotel, maybe they had a fund for the kids of their employees," my mom went on. "But there was nothing. I didn't know what to do. Then it was yesterday, and I panicked."

"That's when she called my office," Crystal stepped in.

"What? Why?"

"I know Crystal is a good person—you know how she

gives cars away on her show and takes audiences on trips and whatnot," my mother explained. "I was out of ideas. I'd even tried your father."

My father.

For a black girl, I must have turned white. My mother hadn't mentioned my dad in years. I didn't know his name. I had no idea she knew where he was. Now my mother was saying that she not only knew where he was, but that she'd called him? I felt ready to cry.

"No," I croaked.

"Ronette, dear, when a person is desperate, they do what they think they have to do," Crystal said gently. Once again, it was as if my mother and I were guests on her show.

"This is not right!" I exclaimed. "She shouldn't have called him. I don't even know him!"

"I called him," my mother repeated. "I had to."

"So what happened?" I demanded.

My mother and Crystal shared a long look.

"Tell her," Crystal instructed.

"He has another family now," my mom explained. "He said it would wreck it if he sent you money. They don't know about you."

I slumped. This was too much to take in. Too much. I was too upset even to cry.

Then I knew what I had to do. About my father, anyway.

I faced her. "I want his number."

"No." My mom's response was immediate.

"Yes. You have to give it to her. "

Omigod. Crystal had just jumped in on my side.

"Kalina," she went on. "Give your daughter his number. She's a college girl now. If she's old enough to hear about him like this, she's old enough to have his phone number." She spun toward me. "Use it wisely."

My mom took out her cell phone and sent me a text. My own cell chimed. My father's number. I didn't recognize the area code. "What his name?" I asked.

"Trenton. Trenton Landry."

It dawned on me that my last name could have been Ronette Landry.

Crystal sipped her tea. "Okay. So that's done. After she called your father, your mother called me. Actually, she called the show. It took a while for the message to work its way to me, but when she said you were at Houseman, and that you were Lori's roommate—she didn't say Lori, she said Chyna—I called her back. She shared the situation. I wanted to meet her before I intervened."

"Crystal flew me to Washington this morning," my mother said proudly. "We had lunch."

"It's just lucky that I'm here. I met your mother. I heard your story. I decided to write a check. Any questions?"

I had one. "Did you talk to Chyna about me?"

"No. Why? I didn't have to."

So, Crystal had made this happen on her own. On the one hand, I had to admire my mother for her initiative. On the other hand, doing this behind my back, and making me believe that there was money for college when there wasn't …

Gawd. Her daughter was so hateful to me. Such a beeyotch. She would hold it over me forever that her mother was paying for my education.

No way. No way in hell.

I stood. "I'm sorry, Crystal, I can't accept your money."

"Ronette!" my mother chided me. "This is not how I raised you!"

I swung hotly toward my mother. "You also didn't raise me to lie about big things, like about having the money for college when you didn't and not knowing where my father was. I am not going to accept this." I turned back to Crystal. "And by the way? Your daughter is a horror show. I wouldn't wish her on anyone."

That was it. I was outta there.

Chapter Seventeen

For the rest of the evening—until well after dark, in fact—I wandered around Dee Cee.

Later, I realized that I must have gone past the Capitol, along the big reflecting pool on the National Mall, and then past the Vietnam Memorial. I have vague memories of people speaking various languages, groups of Asian visitors with smartphones and cameras, and clusters of school kids wearing identical T-shirts.

My memories are thin. Though I was moving, I was barely aware of my footsteps. Though seeing, I did not register what was before my eyes. Though my ears could hear, I was not listening. There must have been happy shouts from children rolling in the grass on the mall, or reverent whispers at the Vietnam Memorial. I just don't remember.

Instead, my head was full of images; my heart rended by emotion. Yet my spirit was numb. I literally hit myself in the forehead with an open hand so I could feel pain. Maybe if it was a bad dream, that would have woken me up.

Crystal had paid my tuition. The mother of my hated roommate. She said that she hadn't talked to Chyna about it, and Chyna had said that she hadn't talked to her. My mother had planned to keep it secret from me. She was going to make it seem like she'd come up with the money. I only got on to the truth because the bursar had flapped her gums.

My mother had talked to my father. That was supposed to be a secret too. I had his digits now and his name. Trenton. Wasn't that the capital of New Jersey? Who names their kid after a place in New Jersey? Whatever his name, he'd made it clear what he thought about me. I was worse than garbage. Once garbage is in the dumpster, it gets taken away. But I was actually dangerous to him. Asshole.

How could I possibly accept the money?

These were my thoughts as I wandered north on Vermont Avenue, like I was heading for Howard University.

At the corner of Vermont and U Street, something got my attention. A monument that I, queen of useless knowledge, must have somehow remembered was there.

It was the monument of four Civil War soldiers. Three were foot soldiers carrying long rifles. The other was obviously a sailor, holding on to the wheel that steered a ship.

These soldiers were all black. At the base of the statue was an inscription: CIVIL WAR TO CIVIL RIGHTS AND BEYOND.

The statue was in the middle of a small plaza. Etched onto the stainless steel of the plaza walls behind were the names of thousands—tens of thousands, maybe hundreds of thousands—of African American soldiers who had fought in the Civil War.

I was the only one there. Even in my own pain, I wondered what those soldiers would say if they could come to life and talk. What was it like to be black and fight for the freedom of slaves in the South? To be descended from a stranger in a strange land, but still to take up arms for your new home? How many of the people listed on the panels had survived and were the great-great-great-grand-parents of kids I knew in Chicago or at Houseman? How many had died one of those horrible Civil War deaths I'd read about where infections ravaged their bodies and the doctors actually made things worse?

Then I had another silent question: If Jayson had been alive back then, would he have volunteered? I thought for sure he would.

Thinking of Jayson brought me back to reality. I hadn't even called him. I needed to go back to Houseman, find him, and talk this out.

I texted, "See you soon. Lotsa news."

I found the U Street Metro stop and took two trains to get to Adams-Morgan. Caught the Houseman shuttle in Adams-Morgan; it dropped me at McMaster. Took the elevator upstairs, and plodded down the hall to my room. There was a red bandana tied around the door handle, but I paid it no heed as I let myself in—

I cursed. Big-time.

I'd walked in on two people in Chyna's bed gettin' busy.

She shouted at me. "Are you stupid or something? Didn't you see the bandana? Get the crap out!"

My intention was to do just that. I mean it. It was. Until I saw the face of the guy underneath her.

Jayson.

Chapter Eighteen

For the second time in six hours, I was sure my eyes were deceiving me. I shook my head to clear my vision. It had to be someone who looked like Jayson, not really Jayson.

No. It was him.

A wave of nausea roiled my guts. I could literally feel my stomach pulse. I was *this close* to making a deposit on Chyna's rug. Then the nausea was gone, replaced by super-conductive fury. My soul froze so cold that a tap on my wrist would have shattered me.

No one would have blamed me if I had killed Jayson right then and there. If I had stabbed him through the heart in the heat of passion, no jury would have convicted me. I was mad-angry enough to do it too. My boyfriend in bed with my detested roommate? This was impossible. But this was a day where the impossible had become real, and I could not dispute the visual evidence.

This scumbag was my first? What was wrong with me?

I said and did nothing to him. Without a word, I moved to my bed. Underneath were the suitcases with which I'd arrived at National Airport just five days before.

"Don't you know what a scarf on the doorknob means, Ronette?" Chyna demanded.

I didn't answer.

"It means, don't come in," she explained. "It means, keep your ass out!"

I wasn't paying attention. I was busy filling my suitcases.

"You came in anyway," she went on.

"I need to talk to Ronette," I heard Jayson say.

"I'm not stopping you," Chyna told him.

"I mean, alone. Can you give us a few minutes?"

Silence from behind me as I slammed clothes in my suitcases. It had taken me two hours to pack to come to college. I was going to pack to depart in two minutes.

"That won't be necessary," I muttered. I couldn't look at him. It would hurt too much.

"Come on, Ronette," Jayson cajoled. "Don't be like that."

"Don't be like what? How you were when I came in

here? I think I am already like that, come to think of it. I got screwed!" I had one suitcase filled. I moved on to the other one.

"I can explain!" His voice was high, almost pleading.

I heard Chyna laugh. "Good luck with that."

Shirts. Jeans. Underwear that would have been too cheap to touch Chyna's perfect body. Each item that went into the second suitcase brought a memory. A Cubs game with Jayson. Seeing Dr. Dre live in Lincoln Park. First date. Second date. Last date.

Then I had the black dress in my hands—the one that Jayson had sent me to wear the night before he left. The fancy dinner. Sitting side by side in the restaurant. Holding hands. The ride to his place. His room. Candles. His guns. His—

No way I was keeping it. I tossed it over my shoulder back toward Jayson and Chyna.

"Ronette …" he said.

My voice got mechanical. "Jayson, the smart thing for you to do would be to just leave now because I do not want to see your face ever again and especially not when I am leaving here. Do that for me please."

Shoes next. Then bathroom stuff. Then I was done. I didn't have a plan other than getting out and never coming back.

"I can explain, Ronette," Jayson pleaded. "It isn't what you think."

Okay. I was a hotel maid. That meant I could take a lot of crap. Yet even a maid knows how to fight back. That hotel clock radio alarm that goes off at three in the morning? It doesn't get set that way by accident.

I picked up my suitcases, slung my backpack over my shoulder, and turned to him.

"Jayson, you have no idea what I think. You are never, ever going to know. Because I am never going to speak to you again or speak of you again. You're dead to me."

I shifted my gaze to Chyna, who'd put on yet another of her silk robes and seemed to be assessing me thoughtfully. "You can have him. Oh, that's right. You already did."

"Open the door."

She didn't move.

"Open the damn door!" I ordered.

This time, she opened it. I stepped through, my suitcases knocking painfully against my legs. I didn't yelp or stumble. I just headed for the elevators. I passed a couple of kids on our floor who stared at me. I had nothing to say. I took the elevator downstairs, strode past the surprised guard, and stepped out into the Dee Cee night.

Now what?

I had plenty of good anger on my side, but no plan. I thought vaguely that I should get back to Chicago. But how? I had no money to pay for a plane ticket.

"Hey, Ronette? Where you goin' with those suitcases?"

It was Marta. As luck would have it, she happened to be passing McMaster at that very moment on her way home from the library. (I found out later that luck had nothing to do with it, but that's a story whose details can wait.)

"I'm leaving," I said.

I decided to walk to the shuttle stop. From there, I could go to Adams-Morgan, and from Adams-Morgan to National Airport. What I'd do at the airport was anyone's guess, but I didn't want to spend one more minute on the campus where my boyfriend had just done it with Chyna.

"Interesting. Do you want to talk about it?" Marta stepped in next to me. For a change, she was wearing a sweat suit instead of one of her tight dresses.

"No."

"Seriously?"

I kept walking.

"Those bags must be heavy," she surmised. "Can I help you with them?"

"I'm fine."

I wasn't fine. My arms felt like they were coming out of my sockets.

"Can I ask what happened?"

"Ask all you want," I told her. "I don't feel like talking."

We walked in silence for a few moments. Then she asked a question I didn't expect.

"Do you need money?"

I shook my head. "No … well, yes. But not from you."

We reached the shuttle stop. I put down my bags.

"I can lend you some," she told me. "But I wish you would tell me what happened. Listen. Let's get a coffee. Or tea. Or something. Okay?" She pointed to the shuttle sign. "The next shuttle isn't for thirty minutes. You can pick it up by the library. If you still want to go, then I'll give you money. Take as long as you want to pay it back. Come on, Ronette."

I understood that I could wait outside the dorm, or I could go with her. If I waited outside the dorm, there was a chance Jayson would come out. I did not want to see him. Did not.

I went with her. We must have looked stupid, lugging my suitcases across campus to the library. Ten minutes later, we were sitting together in the Grind. Marta got herself a coffee and me a juice.

"So," she said after she sat down. "Talk."

I talked. And talked. And talked.

I started with Shaaban Lowe's class and went through

my visit to the bursar. My showdown with Chyna. Then the incredible meeting with Crystal and my mother. My walk around Washington, and the stop at the Civil War monument. And finally, finding my boyfriend in bed with my loathsome roommate.

It took a lot longer than a half hour. Marta listened carefully, nodding a lot, wincing at my description of Jayson and Crystal.

"That's why I'm leaving," I concluded. "I don't belong here. No way am I letting her mother pay for me to be here."

She nodded, then took a long swallow of her coffee. "I get it, girlfriend. I do."

"Thank you for understanding."

"I've got cash in my room," Marta promised.

I was so grateful. I'd expected to be judged, but Marta wasn't judging me.

"Your mouth must be worn out. Drink your juice," my friend instructed.

I touched my dry lips with my tongue. She was right. Juice would be good.

"My parents weren't born in America, you know," she told me. "They're immigrants. Many years ago, the leader of Cuba was disgusted with the people who didn't appreciate communism."

"Fidel Castro, you mean," I filled in.

"Exactly. He decided he'd be better off without them. Of course, he wasn't going to buy them plane tickets. He let them go by boat. Or raft. Whatever they could find. He sent the criminals and the crazies too."

"You're talking about the Mariel boatlift," I remarked. I still felt horrible, but it wasn't quite so bad now that Marta knew.

"That's right. How do you know that?"

I tapped my head with my forefinger. "I know a ton of useless stuff. But nothing useful, like that my boyfriend was going to cheat on me."

"Let's stay with the boatlift," Marta urged. "Anyway, my mom and dad, they were on two of those rafts. They were just kids. My mom's got here fine. But my dad was the only survivor on his. My grandparents—*mis abuelos*— ended up in the sea."

"Oh my God," I exclaimed.

"I don't think God had anything to do with it," she said. "At least, I hope not." She leaned toward me. "Here's my point. You're here. You've got an opportunity here. It may not be happening the way you want, but it wasn't the way my father wanted it to be either. Meanwhile, he took it and made something of it."

Okay. I was so grateful for her friendship. And Marta had meant that to be inspirational. I loved her for that. But all it did was make me sad. Especially when I thought about my visit to the monument.

"It's not the same," I told her wearily. "At least your mom and dad came here voluntarily. My ancestors came here in chains. You know who your people are. Most of the kids at this school? They don't know nothing. Do you know how it crushes you to not know who you are or where you come from?"

Marta was silent for a long time after that. Then she showed the kind of character that made me want her to be my friend.

"You're right. It's not the same," she agreed. "But just like my parents, you gotta play the hand you got."

"That's what I'm doing," I told her. "I hear when you get a crap hand, the best thing is to throw in your cards and go home."

"True," Marta allowed. "But let me tell you what's going to happen after you leave. You think you're making a statement? To your mother, and your boyfriend, and Chyna, and Crystal? Five minutes after you're gone, no one is going to remember you. Except for me and maybe Shaaban Lowe." She stood. "I don't know about you, but

I can't do a heavy yak for more than forty-five minutes without a break. Let me know what you want to do. If you do leave? I'm going to be really sad. Keep me posted."

She hugged me. I hugged her back. Then she left me alone.

I sat there with my suitcases and my juice and thought about what to do.

Chapter Nineteen

"*Who's* there?"

Chyna was in the bathroom when I dropped my suit-cases on the floor of my dorm room with a loud thud.

I didn't answer. I owed her nothing.

She flung the door open suspiciously. She was wearing yet another robe. This one was black and sheer. What did she do? Buy them by the dozen?

"Oh. It's you," she muttered. "I was hoping you were gone for good."

"Which is exactly why I'm back."

I put my suitcases on my bed and started to unpack. There were a bunch of reasons I'd decided to stay, one of which was that I wasn't finished with Lori Williams-also-known-as-Chyna. But the biggest reason was that I didn't have much of a life to go back to. I would have ended up cleaning hotel rooms at the Apex and attending CCC. Plus, if you took Chyna and Jayson out of the equation, I knew Houseman was the right place for me. I had a new soul friend in Marta. I had a teacher I admired in Shaaban Lowe. I was learning how to study for the first time in my life. I was into the Dee Cee, with its quirky neighborhoods, its monuments and history.

When I'd called Marta to share my decision, she'd screamed with happiness.

"He loves you, you know." Chyna's words pulled me out of my musings.

I laughed coldly. "I'm so sure."

"No, seriously," she said. She sat on her bed and crossed her long, lean legs. For the first time, I noticed her fancy gold star-patterned pedicure. The stars looked like they were made of gold leaf. "You should ask him."

"If that's love, I'm not interested. He's all yours." I dug out my boring shoes and put them under my bed.

"True. If I wanted him. Which I don't. He's got some nice guns, though."

Did she have to bring that up?

"Whatever."

Underwear. T-shirts. Jeans. Sweaters. I unpacked

methodically, wishing that this girl who had just hit it with my boyfriend—ex-boyfriend—would shut up.

"You should fight for him," she advised me.

I whirled. I'd had enough of her bull.

"I don't need your advice about how to live, Chyna. From what I can tell, you've messed up your life pretty good. You're in and out of rehab the way most girls are in and out of the bathroom. You hit it with other girls' boyfriends. You steal other people's work and pass it off as your own. By the way, you should burn my notebook. I've got my other poems on my computer, and it's backed up to the Cloud. You so much as a rap a single line I've written, it'll be on the home page of TMZ."

I stopped for a moment, then realized I had one more thing to say.

"Oh. About being roommates? If you don't like living with me? Leave. Because I'm staying."

For the first time, it looked like I'd gotten to her. She raised a finger as if she wanted to say something to me, then changed her mind. Instead, she got dressed in black leggings and a short white pullover, tugged on some flats, and wordlessly left the room.

I was alone with my empty suitcases. I took them off the bed and stowed them underneath. Then I kicked off my shoes, sprawled on my bed, and booted up my laptop. I wanted to write. There was no reason I couldn't type it, the way real writers did.

I got my title right away.

"In da House"

Out go da lights
You think everything all right
You close your eyes, go beddy-bye
Pray to God you fall asleep
What you don't know's the devil
In da house ...

It was a decent start, but I wasn't sure where to go with it. Then I understood why. There were a lot of devils in my house. My mom. Jayson. Crystal. Chyna. My father. I couldn't really be myself until I'd exorcised them.

Time to do just that.

I took out my cell. Almost midnight. The person I was calling would probably be sleeping. I punched in the number.

"Hello?"

"Hello," I said in my firmest voice. "This is Ronette. We need to talk."

❧ 158 ❧

JEFF GOTTESFELD

*J*eff Gottesfeld is a best-selling, award-winning writer for page, screen, and stage. His *Robinson's Hood* trilogy for Saddleback won the "IPPY" Silver Medal for multicultural fiction for teens; he also was part of the editorial team on *Juicy Central*. He was Emmy-nominated for his work on the CBS daytime drama *The Young and the Restless*, and also wrote for *Smallville* and *As the World Turns*. His *Anne Frank and Me* (as himself) and *The A-List* series (as Zoey Dean) were NCSS and ALA award-winning *Los Angeles Times* and *New York Times* bestsellers. Coming soon is his first picture book, *The Tree in the Courtyard*. He was born in Manhattan, went to school in Maine, has lived in Tennessee and Utah, and now happily calls Los Angeles home. He speaks three languages, and thinks all teens deserve to find the fun in great stories. Learn more at www.jeffgottesfeldwrites.com.